THE UNSEEN

ROY JACOBSEN

THE UNSEEN

Translated from the Norwegian by
Don Bartlett and Don Shaw

MACLEHOSE PRESS
QUERCUS · LONDON

Co-funded by the
Creative Europe Programme
of the European Union

This publication has been funded with support from the European Commission.
This publication reflects the views only of the author, and the Commission cannot be held
responsible for any use which may be made of the information contained therein.

This translation has been published with the financial support of NORLA

A CIP catalogue record for this book is available
from the British Library

ISBN (MMP) 978 1 84866 610 8
ISBN (Ebook) 978 1 84866 609 2

2 4 6 8 10 9 7 5 3 1

Designed and typeset by Libanus Press in Adobe Caslon
Printed and bound in Great Britain by Clays Ltd, St Ives plc

1

On a windless day in July the smoke rises vertically to the sky. Pastor Johannes Malmberget is rowed out to the island and received by the fisherman-cum-farmer Hans Barrøy, the island's rightful owner and head of its sole family. He stands on the landing place his forefathers constructed with rocks from the shore and watches the incoming *færing*, the bulging backs of the two oarsmen and, behind their black cloth caps, the smiling, freshly shaven face of the priest. When they have come close enough he shouts:

"Well, well, hier come th' gentry."

Malmberget clambers to his feet and surveys the shore and meadows that stretch up to the houses in the little clump of trees, listens to the screams of seagulls and black-backs that honk like geese on every crag along the coast, to the terns and the strutting waders that bore into the snow-white beaches beneath the radiant sunlight.

But when he scrambles out of the *færing* and teeters a few steps along the mole he catches sight of something he has never seen before, his home on the main island the way it looks from Barrøy, along with the Trading Post and the buildings, the farmsteads, the strips of woodland and the fleet of small boats.

"My word, hvur bitty it is. A can scarce see th' houses."

Hans Barrøy says:

"Oh, A can see 'em aright."

"Tha's better eyesight than mysel' then," the priest says, staring over at the community he has worked in for the last thirty years, but has never seen before from such a novel vantage point.

"Well, tha's never been hier afore."

"It's a good two hours' rowin'."

"Has tha no sails?" Hans Barrøy says.

"The's no wind," the priest says, his eyes still trained on his home, but the truth is he is petrified of the sea, and is still trembling and elated to be alive after the calm crossing.

The oarsmen have taken out their pipes and are sitting with their backs turned to them, smoking. At last the priest can shake Hans Barrøy's hand and as he does so he spots the rest of the family who have come down from the houses: Hans's old father, Martin, a widower since his wife passed away almost ten years ago, Hans's unmarried and much younger sister, Barbro. And the woman who reigns on the island, Maria, holding three-year-old Ingrid by the hand, all in their Sunday best, the priest notes with satisfaction, they must have seen the boat when it was rounding Oterholmen, which is now no more than a black hat floating on the sea to the north.

He walks towards the little flock, which has stopped and stands there studying the grass, whereafter he shakes hands with each of them in turn, not one of them ventures to look up, not even old Martin, he has removed his red woolly hat, and finally Ingrid who, the priest observes, has clean white hands, not even black fingernails, which have not been bitten down either, but are neatly trimmed, and look at those small dimples where the knuckles will eventually appear. He stands still, beholding this little work of art and reflecting that soon it will be a hard-working woman's hand, a sinewy, soil-blackened and calloused hand, a man's hand, one of those pieces of wood all hands become here, sooner or later, he says:

"Ah, so their tha is, my dear. Does tha believe in God?"

Ingrid does not answer.

"Indeid she does," says Maria, who is the first to look straight at the guest. But suddenly he makes his initial discovery once again, whereupon he takes a few determined paces past the boat shed, which rises like a step from the water, and makes his way up a hillock from where the view is even better.

"By Jove, A can see th' rectory too."

Hans Barrøy walks past him and says:

"And from hier tha can see th' church."

The priest hurries after him and stands admiring the white-washed church that emerges and looks like a faded postage stamp beneath the black mountains where a few remaining patches of snow resemble teeth in a rotten mouth.

They walk up further, discussing christenings and fish, and

eider down, and the priest waxes lyrical about the island of Barrøy, which from his home looks no more than a black rock on the horizon, but turns out to be the greenest garden, he has, in the name of God, to concede, as are many of the islands out here inhabited by only one or two families, he supposes, Stangholmen, Sveinsøya, Lutvær, Skarven, Måsvær, Havstein, a handful of people on each, who cultivate a thin layer of earth, fish the depths of the sea and bear children that grow up and cultivate the same plots of land and fish the same depths; this is no bleak, infertile coast, rather a string of pearls and a gold necklace, which he is wont to stress in his most inspired sermons. The question is why he doesn't come here more often?

And the answer is the sea.

The priest is a landlubber, and few days in the year are like this, he has been living in dread of it all summer. But standing here at the foot of a grass-covered barn bridge looking into his eternal parish, where God has stood His ground since the Middle Ages, he suddenly realises he hasn't known what it looks like, until now, it is vexing, as though he has had a veil in front of his eyes all these years, as though he has been the victim of a lifelong swindle, with regard to the size of not only his fold but possibly also that of his spiritual mission, is this really all there is to it?

Fortunately, the thought is more unsettling than threatening, metaphysics from the sea where all distances deceive, and he is on the point of losing focus again, but here comes the family – the old man now with the woolly hat on his head, stately Maria right behind him and robust Barbro, whom the priest in the past was unable to confirm, for various and very unclear reasons – God's silent children on a small island in the sea, which in fact turns out to be a jewel.

He begins to discuss the forthcoming christening with them, that of three-year-old Ingrid with the long, tarry-brown hair and bright eyes, and feet that probably won't see a pair of shoes before October; where did she get those eyes, so devoid of that lethargic stupidity engendered by poverty?

In the same euphoric breath he announces that he would like to hear Barbro sing at the christening, she has such a wonderful voice, as far as he remembers . . .

And a flush of embarrassment spreads through the family.

Hans Barrøy draws the priest aside and explains that Barbro has a good voice, yes, but she doesn't know the words of these hymns, she only makes noises she thinks sound right, and they usually are, but that was also the reason she wasn't confirmed, among other reasons, which the priest can probably remember.

Johannes Malmberget drops the matter, but there is another question he would like to take up with Hans Barrøy, concerning the cryptic epitaph, a line of poetry inscribed on Hans's mother's headstone in accordance with her wishes, that has bothered him ever since she was buried in his churchyard, it is not appropriate on a gravestone, it is ambiguous and seems to proclaim that life is not worth living. But as Hans is not very forthcoming about this either, the priest returns to the subject of duck down and whether they have any to sell, he needs two new eiderdowns in his house and is willing to pay more than they would get at the market or Trading Post, down is worth its weight in gold, as they say out here . . .

At last they have something to talk about which is down to earth and as clear as day, and go into the farmhouse where Maria has laid a cloth on the table in the parlour, and after a *lefse* pancake, coffee and a mutually acceptable deal the priest relaxes, feeling that now the greatest mercy which can befall him is sleep, whereupon his eyelids close and his breathing becomes heavier and more protracted. He is sitting in Martin's rocking chair with his hands in his lap, a priest asleep in their home, it is both an impressive and a ridiculous sight. They stand and sit around him until he opens his eyes and chomps his chops and gets up seemingly unaware of where he is. But then he recognises the family and bows. As if to say thank you. They don't know what he is thanking them for, and he says not a word as they follow him down to the boat and watch him lie on a pile of fishing nets in the stern clutching a sack of down and a small barrel of gulls' eggs, only to close his eyes again. As he leaves them, he appears to be asleep. The smoke is still a vertical column to the sky.

2

Everything of value on an island comes from outside, except for the earth, but the islanders are not here because of the earth, of this they are painfully aware. Now Hans Barrøy has broken his last snath and he has to pause from making hay. He can't whittle a new one from materials on the island because it ought to be ash, which he can buy at the Trading Post; alternatively he can use some other type of wood he can find himself, at no cost.

He smacks the scythe blade into the top of a hay-rack pole and strides down the grassy path to the landing place, pushes the *færing* out into the emerald sea, and is about to climb in when he changes his mind, and walks up to the houses instead, where Maria is sitting against the south-facing wall patching a pair of trousers, she looks up as he rounds the corner.

"Hvar's the lass?" he says in an exaggeratedly loud voice, for he knows Ingrid has seen him and hidden so that he will come looking for her and then swing her round and round by the arms. Maria nods in the direction of the potato cellar to indicate her whereabouts. After which, Ingrid's father announces in the same loud voice that she won't be able to go over to Skogshol-men with him then, whereupon he sets off towards the shore. He gets no more than a few metres, though, before he hears her steps behind him, then crouches down at just the right moment so that she can jump up onto his back and fling her arms around his neck and whoop as he races down the hill like a horse, making noises he produces only when the two of them are alone together.

That laugh of hers.

He asks whether they should take the sheepskin.

"Yes," she says, clapping her hands.

He goes into the boat shed to fetch one of the skins and spreads it out in the stern of the *færing* so it resembles a bed, wades ashore again and carries her on board. She nestles down on it, her back against the stern, so she can watch him rowing, look over the gunwale, turn her head from side to side, her small fingers hanging like white lugworms over the tarred, dark brown sides of the boat.

That laugh.

He rows round the headland, through the myriad of islets and skerries, and chooses the direct route to Skogsholmen, as he chunters on about the christening three weeks ago, the church that was so sumptuously decorated for the children from the surrounding islands, all eight of them, and how she was the only one who could walk up to the font on her own legs and say her name when the priest asked what the child was to be called, her father points out that she is getting too big to be lying there like a corpse on a sheepskin instead of doing something useful, rowing or holding a line so that they can take back a pollack or two and not just the raw materials for a new scythe.

She answers that she doesn't want to get bigger, and hangs over first one and then the other gunwale, despite his telling her to sit upright in the boat. He changes his bearings from Oterholmen to the rowan tree at the southern point of Moltholmen, then shifts course again after eighty strokes and rows between the Lundeskjære skerries at the exact point where the water is deep enough at this time of day, before backing an oar and turning the boat into the gap between the rocks on the landward side of the islet, where he has hammered an iron peg into the bare rock.

He tells her to go ashore with the mooring rope, and she stands still holding the boat like a tethered cow while he gets to his feet and looks around, as if there is anything to look at, the birds in the sky, the mountains over there on the mainland beyond his own Barrøy, and the intense screeching of the terns, white and black flashes criss-crossing the air above them.

He steps onto land and shows her how to tie a clove hitch. She can't do it and loses her temper, he shows her again, they tie it together, she laughs, a half-hitch around a peg. He says she can paddle in the rock pool while he goes into the woods, there are too many insects in there.

"Remember t' teik off tha clout."

In the spinney at the bottom of the valley running north to south he finds four straight trunks, not ash, but a type of tree which by rights should not be growing so far north, one of them with a crook just above the base, which will fit snugly against his shoulder, it is more than he could have wished for.

He slings the wood over his shoulder, tramps back up the hillside and slumps down by the rock pool, where she is sitting with water up to her armpits looking at her hands, intertwining her fingers and smacking them down against the surface, causing the rainwater to splash up into her face and making her grimace and howl with glee, that laugh. And his disquiet, which has been there ever since she was born.

He leans back and rests his shoulders against the jagged rock face, his head touching stone, lies there staring up at the swarm of terns listening to her asking questions like any other child, she wants him to join her, the splashing sounds and the cool easterly wind, the salt on his lips, the sweat and the sea, he descends into a whirl of light and darkness, and re-emerges, squinting at her as she stands there stark naked in the sunlight, and she asks if she can dry herself on his clothes.

"Teik this," he says, ripping off his shirt. He hears her laugh at how white his body is, yet black as coal on his arms and neck, he looks like the doll he made for her with parts that don't fit together, this too a normal childish fancy, the doll's name is Oscar, sometimes it is Anni.

On the way back they catch three pollack, which lie next to each other at her feet as she huddles up in his shirt. He says he wants it back as it is cooler now with the evening drawing in. She falls backwards onto the sheepskin, wraps her arms around her calves and looks at him teasingly over her kneecaps.

"Tha laughs at ev'rythin' nu," he says, reflecting that she knows the difference between play and earnest, she seldom cries, doesn't disobey or show defiance, is never ill, and she learns what she needs to, this disquiet he will have to drive from his mind.

"Aren't tha goen' t' get started on 'em?" he says, nodding in the direction of the fish.

"They're vile."

"Hvar did tha learn that word?"

"From Mamma."

"That mamma of thas is a bit la-di-da. We're not, ar' we?"

She thinks about this, with two fingers in her mouth.

"Th' gulls are starvin'," she says.

She inserts her right hand into the belly of the biggest pollack, tears out the guts and holds them aloft with disgust in her eyes. He rows on, changing bearings as he goes, she hurls the guts over the side and watches the seagulls swoop down for them and splash and eat and fight in a kind of life-and-death struggle. She sticks her hand into the next fish, flings the guts over the birds, and then digs into the last one, leans over the gunwale and rinses the fish one by one, places them side by side on the floorboards, the biggest to starboard, the second biggest in the middle, and the small one to port, washes her hands, slowly and thoroughly, there are no flaws in this child's mind he decides with his eyes half-closed, as he feels from the lie of the boat that she is still hanging over the side, she is drawing squiggles in the water, so he has to row a heeling boat home, he drags it only halfway up the landing place and jams the trestles under the gunwales, because the tide is going out.

She walks in front of him up the path, dragging the catch with the last drops of blood running down her slender calves. On his shoulders the four lengths of wood, the axe under his arm, in his hand her dry clothes. He stops and looks at the sun in the north-west, it has become pale and hazy and will soon be a moon, night is approaching, and he wonders whether to repair the scythe at once or get a few hours' sleep before the dew falls in Rose Acre next morning; the dew always forms first in Rose Acre, where a strange red grass grows.

3

Whatever is washed ashore on an island belongs to the finder, and the islanders find a lot. It might be cork or barrels or hemp or driftwood or flotage – green and brown glass balls to stop fishing nets sinking – which old Martin Barrøy disentangles from the piles of seaweed when the storm has blown over, then sits down in the boat shed to fasten new nets around, making them look like new. There might be a wooden toy for Ingrid, there might be fish boxes and oars, gaffs, bow rollers, bailers, poles, planks and the remains of boats. One winter night a whole wheelhouse was washed ashore. They used the horse to drag it onto dry land and left it there in the south of the island so that Ingrid could sit in the skipper's swivel chair and turn the brass and mahogany wheel as she looked out over the meadows and stone walls that roll like waves across the island.

There are no fewer than eight walls.

They have been built of stones which rise through the earth like the glass floats in the sea, only much more slowly, it takes many winters for them to work their way up, they can collect the stones in the spring and make the walls even higher, these walls which divide the island into nine sections, or acres as they call them. South Acre is the most exposed, the sea crashes in here, with all its brutality. Then comes Bosom Acre, nobody knows how it got its name, but it might be because of the conical green haystacks and grass-strewn patches of protruding rock resembling large and small breasts, which the sheep chew at until they are nice and round after the haymaking is done. Next is Stone Acre, since it has more stones than the others, then Rose Acre because the grass there is as red as unripe rowanberries. Cowbarn Acre surrounds the buildings, the Garden of Eden faces north, but is nonetheless the most fertile, this is where the potato fields always are, then comes Scab Acre, North Acre and Needy Acre, which all have well-deserved names, even though Needy Acre is the greenest of them all and envelops the boat shed and the landing place like a thick green mitten.

But mostly they find rubbish.

They find dead porpoises and auks and cormorants full to bursting with stinking gases, they wade through rotting seaweed and find parts of shoes and a hat and an armband and a crutch and fragments of distant lives, testimony to opulence, laxity, loss and carelessness, and misfortune which has befallen people they have never heard of and will never meet. Now and then they also stumble across objects with stories behind them that they can never know, a coat with pockets full of newspapers and tobacco from England, a wreath on a watery grave, the French tricolour on a splintered flagpole and a slimy casket containing an exotic woman's most intimate possessions.

On rare occasions they find a message in a bottle, a mixture of longing and personal confidences intended for others than the finders, but which, if they were to have reached the intended recipient, would have caused them to weep tears of blood and move all heaven and earth. Now, in all their indifference the islanders open the bottles, pick out the letters and read them, if they understand the language they are written in, that is, and reflect on the contents, superficial, vague reflections – messages in bottles are mythical vehicles of yearning, hope and unfulfilled lives – and then they put the letters in a chest reserved for objects which can neither be possessed nor discarded, and boil the bottles and fill them with redcurrant juice, or else simply place them on the windowsill in the barn as a kind of proof of their own emptiness, leaving the sunbeams to shine through them and turn green before refracting downwards and settling in the dry straw littering the floor.

But one autumn morning Hans Barrøy finds a whole tree that the storm has torn up and deposited on the southern tip of the island. An enormous tree. He can't believe his eyes.

Now the sea, in company with the wind, is calming down, and the tree lies there like the skeleton of a prehistoric monster, a whale carcass, with roots and branches intact, but devoid of needles and bark, the sea has consumed these, a ton of white resin, so useful all over the world as it can be used to coat the bows of famous violinists, enabling them to produce rich, pure tones. It is a Russian larch which through the centuries has grown strong and mighty on the banks of the Yenisei in the wilds south of Krasnoyarsk, where the winds that rage across the *taiga* have left their mark like a comb in greasy hair, until the time when a spring flood with teeth of ice toppled the tree into the river and transported it three or four thousand kilometres north to the Kara Sea and left it in the clutches of its briny currents, which carried it north to the edge of the ice and then west past Novaya Zemlya and Spitsbergen and all the way up to the coasts of Greenland and Iceland, where warmer currents wrested it from their grip and drove it north-west again, in a mighty arc halfway around the earth, taking in all a decade or two, until a final storm swept it onto an island on the Norwegian coast, where early one morning in October it is found by Hans Barrøy, who gapes at it in disbelief.

A mightier tree has never been observed in these parts.

He runs home to fetch his family.

They set about dismembering the quarry, they lop off and saw up the roots and branches and stack them against the north wall of the barn, to be used as kindling, then pitch into the trunk itself, log by log. But suddenly they are confronted with a Roman column of solid wood, around thirteen metres in length, and, even using the horse and a pulley system together with the combined efforts of five people they can't move it up to the farm. They secure it with a rope and go home and sleep on the problem, exhausted, empty and content. And at the next tide they manoeuvre it higher up, a few more metres, but there it remains, a fallen marble pillar.

Hans and Martin cut off two more sections, it takes them a

whole day, and they see that the resin-rich heartwood becomes redder and redder, the closer to the core they get, as hard as glass yet still amenable to the blade. They scrape it off and rub it between their fingers and breathe in the smell, which makes them realise that it is impossible to cut up this magnificent specimen only to burn it in a stove. The tree is an organic whole which has to be preserved, one day they will find a use for it, who knows when, or they will be able to sell it, it must be worth a fortune.

With one final burst of energy they roll it up onto three skids so that it is clear of the grass, hammer four posts into the ground on either side, then drive iron pegs through them and into the wood. And there this pillar lies today, one hundred years later, a great white cylinder beside the sea. One might think someone has forgotten all about it, it might look as though it once had some function, as if in days gone by it had been indispensable.

4

Nobody can leave an island. An island is a cosmos in a nutshell, where the stars slumber in the grass beneath the snow. But occasionally someone tries. And on such a day a gentle easterly wind is blowing. Hans Barrøy has hoisted the sail, a weather-beaten fore-and-aft rig, and it proves to be a fine crossing over to the Trading Post. The whole family has come along, except for old Martin, he has no faith in this venture.

They are going to part company with Barbro. Barbro is twenty-three and the time has come for her to take up a position as a housemaid, they have found a place for her.

After they have moored the boat beneath the wharf at the Trading Post Ingrid leads her up to the General Store and the village, where the trees reach up to the sky and the houses are painted and so close together that you can go from one to the other without a coat on.

Barbro won't hold hands with anybody except Ingrid, because she knows what is going to happen, she stops in front of the shop, with all eyes staring at them, these islanders, they are so rarely seen here. Ingrid is wearing a blue dress and a grey cardigan adorned with green ice crystals on the collar and sleeves. Barbro is attired in a yellow dress and a wadmal jacket that is too short for her, she says she wants some rock sugar.

Hans has caught them up and says yes, she can have some. But, when they come out of the Store, Barbro doesn't want to go on to the farmstead where the lady of the house, Gretha Sabina Tommesen, has agreed to take her in as a housemaid on condition that it will cost her no more than the price of food and a bed. Hans and Maria have to drag her there, while Ingrid brings up the rear of the procession and casts stolen glances at the herd of children following them at a distance. She has seen some of them before, briefly, at church or the Store, she knows the names of two of them, recognises four other faces, but none of them is smiling, and she doesn't stare for long, she runs after the others into the garden surrounding the white house, which has a heavy, dark panelled door that opens and admits them into another world.

But then Gretha Sabina Tommesen manages to call Barbro "the imbecile" three times as she shows them the room Hans's sister is to share with the other maid, who is also from the islands, only much younger than Barbro. The mistress of the house explains that the imbecile also has to reckon on being called down to the Post when the herring boats come in, even in the middle of the night, just like the other women in the house.

"Can she gut?"

"Oh, yes," Maria replies. "She can cook, too, an' card an' spin an' knit stockin's."

"Is she clean?"

"Tha can see that."

"Do you understand what I'm saying, Barbro?" she shouts at Barbro, who nods and gazes up at a crystal chandelier hanging above her head, a starry firmament her eyes sink so deeply into that they remain there, and her neck locks. When Gretha Sabina Tommesen then tells Maria that her sister-in-law cannot expect to be supplied with any more clothes than those she has brought with her, Hans looks at his sister – who is still standing with her eyes fixed on the new solar system – and makes a decision, takes her in one hand and the small suitcase in the other and strides out of the house, once again making his way to the Store, where he waits for Maria and Ingrid to catch them up. The husband and wife look at each other. He nods towards the door. She nods back. They go in for a second time and buy sugar and coffee, two packets of four-inch nails, a bucket of tar, some pearl sago, cinnamon, a barrel of coarse salt, and also order three large sacks of rye flour, to be collected in four days, then leave the Store, go down to the wharf again with their purchases, climb aboard the *færing* and set sail.

A fair wind takes them home.

Hans can't look at his sister, Barbro. He sits on the opposite side of the tiller so the sail is between them. But this does not mean that he has escaped Maria's gaze, she is twenty-seven years old, strong and comes from another island, she has attended a home economics school and could have found a placement anywhere, but she is on Barrøy, with him, Hans Barrøy, who is thirty-five and here he is, hiding from his own sister and a vexing sense of shame, they are two sides of the same coin, the shame and the hiding place, but still he is exposed to Maria's eye, it does not relent until he admits he has been a fool, a nod is sufficient. Then she diverts her gaze to the waves and adopts that irritating smile, which makes her even more indomitable.

Old Martin is waiting on the beach and receives them with a guffaw.

"Hva did A tell tha!"

He wades out and carries the suitcase ashore, then leads his daughter up to the house with Ingrid running alongside telling him about the visit until her voice is drowned by the shrieks of the gulls. Maria and Hans stay at the landing place discussing whether to fetch the cart or carry the goods up to the house in their arms.

"It's not too much f'r us t' carry, is it?"

She leads the way. He drops what he is carrying, grabs her by the hips and pulls her down into the tall grass, where not even God can see them, nor hear her half-stifled cries, and she calls him all kinds of names as her smile reappears, the smile that only a short while ago she shot at the waves, he has as good as brought it back to her lips. And afterwards they have no desire to resume their homeward trek, they lie there on their backs staring at the sky as she tells him about her childhood at home on Buøy, a cowshed collapsed as a result of too much snow on one side of the roof. He listens and wonders where this is leading, as he always does, what is Maria thinking and what is she getting at? Until Ingrid is suddenly looking down at them, asking hvar they've been, Barbro wants to know what they are having for supper, herring or pollack or the halibut her father caught in his seine net yesterday.

"A'll see t' th' halibut," Hans says, getting up, and he fetches the cart after all and loads it with the things they bought at the Store, and Ingrid, and wheels it up the hill while Maria stays put. She is the philosopher on the island, the one with the oblique way of looking at things, since she comes from a different island and has something to compare with, this might be termed experience, wisdom even, but it can also give her a split personality, it depends on how different the eyes or the islands are.

5

They have three sallow trees on Barrøy, four birches and five rowans, of which one is scarred and as big as a barrel around the middle and is called the Old Rowan, and all twelve lean in the direction nature has bent them.

There are also some smaller, wispy birch trees on a crag to the west, they stand as if embracing one another and are known as Kjærlighetslund, Love Spinney, but spread out in all directions when the wind blows.

In addition, they have a hefty sallow tree which seems to lie along the ground and has existed like this for as long as anyone can remember, on its knees, on the boundary between Rose Acre and Bosom Acre. Their forefathers built the stone wall around it rather than cut it down. It is presumably the only tree on the island that cannot be felled. Not that they would fell the others either, even though wood is both precious and necessary, so the thought does occasionally cross their minds. But no-one ever considers chopping down the sallow on the boundary between the two Acres, in a way it has already been felled where it is, and is thereby consecrated, like a grave.

From the largest rowans around the houses hang large

magpie nests. The islanders often curse the magpies because they steal and shit, and they talk about destroying their nests. But that doesn't happen either. So when the immense constructions in the branches sway in the battle against yet another storm and survive once again, the islanders observe with stoic relief that nothing has been damaged this time either, although often enough this is not the case.

On the very rare occasions the rain or snow falls vertically, a dry circle forms in the grass beneath every nest in the Old Rowan. Then the sheep huddle together there. Especially the lambs dislike the rain, and they relieve themselves as animals do, so there is a black, muddy circle of life beneath every nest, everything is interconnected, just as humans do not divide into two separate parts even though they bend forward.

This is how it is on the thousand other islands in the archipelago as well.

The ten thousand islands.

As the terrain is so open and exposed someone might well come up with the bright idea of clothing the coast in evergreens, spruce or pines for example, and establish idealistic nurseries around Norway and start to ship out large quantities of tiny spruce trees, donating them free of charge to the inhabitants of smaller and bigger islands alike, while telling them that if you plant these trees on your land and let them grow, succeeding generations will have fuel and timber too. The wind will stop blowing the soil into the sea, and both man and beast will enjoy shelter and peace where hitherto they had the wind in their hair day and night; but then the islands would no longer look like floating temples on the horizon, they would resemble neglected wastelands of sedge grass and northern dock. No, no-one would think of doing this, of destroying a horizon. The horizon is probably the most important resource they have out here, the quivering optic nerve in a dream although they barely notice it, let alone attempt to articulate its significance. No, nobody would even consider doing this until the country attains such wealth that it is in the process of going to rack and ruin.

6

It is spring again and the sky is high above the islands, the winds are cold and confused and bring along gusts of warm air. The oystercatchers have returned to the beach and strut about like black-and-white chickens, nodding their heads and boring their long red bills into the sand, drilling and drilling and cheep-cheeping, unable to do anything else, oystercatchers are idiotic birds, but they come with spring.

In mid-fjord the wind suddenly drops.

Hans Barrøy has to lower the sail and start rowing. Maria grabs the oars too, sits down behind him and keeps jabbing him in the back with her knuckles until he shouts stop, that hurts, and womenfolk . . . know next t' bloody nothin' about rowin'. Barbro and Ingrid, squeezed into blue and yellow dresses, laugh, sitting on a sheepskin in the stern with a little suitcase and the idle tiller between them.

"Tha's not rowin' straight."

"A am that," Maria says, resting one oar so the *færing* veers to the side. Barbro laughs again even though she knows what is going to happen, the same as last time, they are going to get rid of her.

They moor by the Trading Post and walk up towards their destination, Hans with the suitcase first, then Barbro and Ingrid hand in hand, and Maria rounding them off, as it were, she too is dressed up today, as though to emphasise the seriousness of it all, their determination, it went so wrong last time, and none of them says a word.

There is another stop at the Store, and rock sugar, then they continue to the rectory where they are received by the priest's wife, Karen Louise Malmberget, who as recently as three years ago was called Husvik and looks strangely young at the side of the priest, Johannes Malmberget, who has contrived to be a widower twice before Karen Louise came into his house and life. She is childless, he isn't, he has five sons, who all attend a seminary in a town somewhere, as if they left for good when they went and have since forgotten where they come from.

Karen Louise is wearing a light-coloured dress and white pinafore, along with stockings and shoes, even though she is indoors. She greets Barbro – shakes her hand – and bids her welcome, and is talkative and light on her feet, as though she has been looking forward to the visit, takes them round the rooms and shows them the furniture and the sewing machine and the iron and explains where Barbro is to sleep, in a light, inviting room on the first floor with wallpaper, a dresser – a small vase on top – and a porcelain chamber pot with a blue stamp on the bottom.

She explains what Barbro has to do.

And it isn't much, it almost seems as if the priest's wife is on the lookout for company in the house, perhaps even a friend, there isn't much difference between their ages. In the white kitchen she stands with a cookery book the size of a Bible in her hands and asks them whether Barbro can read.

None of them answers.

Karen Louise apologises and says it was stupid of her to ask, flicks through to the section about jam and starts talking about what Barbro will be making, pointing through the window to an army of variously sized fruit bushes lined up in six straight columns down towards a white picket fence at the far end of the garden, still brown after the winter, blackcurrant, redcurrant, gooseberry, and raspberry over there by the rock, which Barbro tells her they have on Barrøy too, they also have redcurrants and she knows how much sugar to put in . . .

At this point Hans Barrøy has to find somewhere to sit.

He plumps down on the chair standing pointlessly between two reception rooms, seemingly there just for decoration, it strikes him that no-one could ever have sat there before. And he doesn't get up again. He leans forward and puts his face in his hands and supports his elbows on his knees as though searching for something in the deepest recesses of his mind, something he is unable to find, when he suddenly senses the others have stopped and are staring at him.

He looks up and says something, he asks where the priest is.

He's in the north of the island, the priest's wife says, some business to attend to . . .

They talk for a while about these people whom Johannes

Malmberget visits and whom, it transpires, Hans knows. When the tour of the house resumes and he is left alone on the pointless chair, he finally finds what he has been searching for, gets up, runs into yet another room after them, takes his sister's hand and drags her into the yard, to wild protests, because Barbro wants to stay in this fine house. The others follow them and stand on the broad stone steps gazing at him in wonderment, Maria shouts something or other, she has an anguished expression on her face.

"A wan' t' be hier," Barbro howls.

"Tha's goen' nohvar," her brother says, manhandling her down to the gate, and bustling her onto the road, where he stands gasping for breath until Maria and Ingrid catch them up. Maria with the suitcase, she asks what the matter is, the same anguished expression on her face, it is almost like grief.

"Nothin'," Hans says.

They walk silently past the Store, there will be no shopping today, continue down to the Trading Post and clamber on board the *færing*. Hans Barrøy observes that the wind has turned and picked up, it is now a south-westerly. He hauls up the sail and struggles to make a sharp tack homeward. Then the rain comes down. Harder and harder the further they get to the mouth of the fjord. Barbro and Ingrid shelter under the sheepskin. There is laughter coming from there anyway, and this time he has no plans to shy away from anyone's gaze, what would be the point, not even from Maria's, she is sitting with her back to the rain, the water running down her brown locks,

33

which become blacker and blacker and resemble fluttering strands of seaweed. And he can find no sign of the smile which usually comes to their rescue.

It sheets down until far into the night, a gale has engulfed them. Reluctantly it veers west and north and becomes colder and less fierce. The sky lightens and the rain no longer lashes the windows as Maria opens her eyes and discovers that the bed beside her is empty. Her hand tells her it is also cold.

She gets up, runs into Barbro and Ingrid's room and instructs them to get dressed and go down with her to the kitchen, where no-one has lit the stove. They ask what is going on. Maria has no answer. They light the stove and eat with Martin, who doesn't speak either, and thereafter go down to the boat shed, where the *færing* is missing. They mend nets with both doors open so that they can always see north, to the Trading Post, the church and the scattered houses, working silently and watchfully and painstakingly, until they finally spot the slanted sail darting up and down in the rough sea like the teeth of a saw, it is the *færing* pitching and tossing on its return, by now evening has fallen.

Hans Barrøy drops sail, the *færing* hits the skids on the shore and comes to a halt. He staggers over two thwarts, bends down in the forepeak and grabs a squirming object, which he heaves ashore, a piglet that immediately runs around squealing in the white shell sand. It cost twelve kroner, has only one ear and a black patch on its forehead like a bullet hole. They can call it whatever they like. He also has some rock sugar in a brown bag, which he hands to Barbro, then he goes into the boat shed for some rope and makes a tether, ties a loop at one end and gives it to Ingrid, who is standing looking down at the piglet, it has started to eat grass.

"That's th' last time tha does that," Maria says, whereupon she turns her back on him and the piglet and walks up to the house to prepare dinner, leaving her husband with a smile on his face, a smile which Ingrid has never seen before. She notices that her mother is angry for the rest of the evening and all next day. But then there is an imperceptible change and the strangeness about her has gone. The piglet is named Grub.

7

The houses on Barrøy stand at an oblique angle to each other. From above they look like four dice someone has thrown at random, plus a potato cellar that becomes an igloo in winter. There are flagstones to walk on between the houses, clothes racks and grass paths radiating in all directions, but actually the buildings act as a wedge against stormy weather so that they can't be flattened, even if the whole sea were to pour over the island.

No-one can claim credit for the ingenious layout of the farmyard, it is the product of collective inherited wisdom, built on bitter experience.

But in the winter time not even a stroke of genius stretching back through the ages can prevent a tidal wave of compact snow settling between the farmhouse and the barn, which they have to struggle through with buckets and milk churns to get to and from the animals. They call it the Wave and curse it like few other phenomena, for the Wave usually surges in when nerves are at their thinnest, in January and February, in December, even in March, a barrier of snow between animals and people, and there is no point shovelling a way through, even though they do, because the snow drifts back straight afterwards. It is the men who shovel and the women who carry the water and milk, so generally there is no alternative for the women but to tramp the whole way round the house and the barn, and it is a long walk when you can't even stand upright in the gusting wind.

But the houses haven't always stood where they stand now, towering up on the highest ridge amidst the clump of trees and fruit bushes, they were once lower down, in a cove a few hundred metres further east called Karvika. There are now only two foundation walls left and the remains of a landing place for boats, which are buried beneath seaweed and sand. And usually no-one thinks about this, the islanders are virtually oblivious to the fact that anyone has ever lived there. But even people who spend their lives tramping on terra firma have moments when they think in less than customary ways and then it strikes you that there must be an explanation for there no longer being any houses in Karvika, what happened to them, these houses, and why aren't they there anymore?

The explanation is doubtless tragic, perhaps horrifying.

Old Martin has been here longest, he is the font of knowledge with the highest status, and of course he has his own opinions about why and when this civilisation came to grief, it concerns his own ancestors, he can also remember some fragments from his childhood, a few images and remnants of conversations and stories. But he is no longer the most trustworthy member of the family, because of his great age and natural degeneration, which not only eats up one's memory, but also brings with it odd ideas and eccentricities that make an old man appear ridiculous in the eyes of the young, every generation goes its own way and remembers only those things it wants to remember. They undoubtedly lead somewhere, these new ways, at worst in the same circles, only to return, it just takes time.

But even though they know nothing at all about the ruins in Karvika, nor the reason why the two houses that were once here no longer are, they still have respect for the ruins. They avoid them, the children don't play in them, the birds don't build nests there, either, not even the common eider, but people don't even consider demolishing them and using the stones for other walls and foundations, for example, those that run between the Acres. They would rather find new stones, so the ruins can remain there like a monument or a cemetery, sinister, overgrown with nettles and willowherb, emanating a sense of something that is both too cold and too warm. If you look at the ruins from the high ground, they resemble two Chinese symbols, written by two different hands. In winter, snow lies on top, making them stand out even more clearly against the brown, decomposing grass, before it too turns white.

8

They have discussed it many times: which room shall we sleep in? In the north-facing one it is perishing cold and uninhabitable when the north-easterlies rage in the winter, but nice and cool in the summer. And virtually silent as the rain generally comes from the south-west, making an infernal racket in the South Chamber no matter whether it is summer or winter. When the summers are particularly wet and they can't dry hay in the fields or on the racks, Hans Barrøy says:

"Right, dear, let's be moven' up north, shall we? We can't stay hier."

When the crystals of ice glisten on the eiderdown cover in winter, he says the opposite, now let's be moven' down south:

"We'll freeze t' death hier."

They take the eiderdowns with them from north to south, and vice versa, allow themselves to be driven by the weather and the seasons since they have a large bed in each of these ceiling-less rooms, which they call bed chambers, the North Chamber and the South Chamber. Ingrid sleeps in the small, west-facing room between these two, which is also sunlit in the middle of the night in the season which they spend the three others dreaming about, and Barbro uses the room facing east, where the good weather comes from.

Old Martin sleeps in a little closet downstairs which is partitioned off from the sitting room. Sometimes he leaves the door open, and he has his own stove, which he keeps well stoked because he is always frozen, so the sitting room is often warm at times of the year when people in this part of the country don't use the sitting room at all, which means that on an ordinary Sunday in October or March the Barrøys can have dinner in there. Then Maria lays a white cloth on the table.

This cloth has narrow borders with tiny flowers, red and yellow, and green vines that connect them, her mother embroidered it, but it is predominantly white.

And Maria prefers to sleep in the South Chamber – even if it is too warm when the weather is good in the summer and it is too noisy in the lousy weather, summer and winter – for from the window here she can see across all of Barrøy and the islets to the south, and on a clear day all the way home to Buøy, where she grew up, her point of comparison. The South Chamber is furthermore a little bigger than the North Chamber, so she can have her chest standing against the wall and also have room for the two bedside tables her father gave them as a wedding present, those pieces of old junk, as he called them; they were originally her mother's, she died all too young, the victim of an epidemic that ravaged the local population with such vehemence that only the strongest survived.

Aren't we goen' t' settle down soon like proper folk, she

says, instead of driften' around like trav'llers?

And after Grub, the piglet, arrives – it is housed in a peat shed which for the moment is empty – Hans feels he has to show some initiative, so when the eider ducks' houses – "th' ei'er huts" – have been repaired and the potatoes have been planted and for a short while the days become longer, milder and more pleasant and they really ought to be cutting peat, he takes along his chisel, sledgehammer and dynamite and walks to the sheer rock face of the cove to the north-west of the island, where tarred posts are sunk vertically into the seabed and bolted to the rock at intervals of half a metre so that medium-sized boats can put in when the weather allows, such as the Trading Post cargo boat or the one belonging to Hans's brother, Erling, who comes by every New Year to pick up Hans and his fishing gear when they go to Lofoten. There is a boat shed here which they call the Lofoten Boathouse, it is closed all year, and contains his valuable Lofoten equipment.

If there is something they really do lack on this island it is a decent quay. So now Old Martin, who has lived quay-less for almost eighty years, is in the farmyard looking north and wondering whether his son is finally going to confront the inevitable, they have been collecting driftwood for a generation, there is no shortage of material.

But Hans Barrøy has other plans. He drills ten deep holes, loads them, primes the fuse and blasts out three cubic metres. The pieces of rock that are too large he smashes with the sledge-hammer.

He walks home for the horse and cart and asks Maria to come with him, explaining to her on the way that he prefers blasted rock for the foundations, it's just a waste of time with those smooth boulders from the beach; blasted rock, on the other hand, has rough surfaces that grip better, then they don't budge an inch. She says:

"Foundations?"

Yes, the solution to the problems of sleep and wind direction is obviously to extend their house to the south, it is a long single-storey building with a loft, ideal for an extension, three or four extra metres will shelter them from the sun and the rain, they can be in the South Chamber all year.

He digs and chops and rakes away a good foot of earth, meets granite and carts in some blasted rock, he is well under way with the project the following day, now with Martin and Barbro's help. Barbro likes hard graft, she grabs a huge lump of rock from the cart, lugs it five paces to where the foundations are and asks her brother where to put it, she won't release it until he indicates the precise position. But he doesn't answer immediately, to tease her, so she goes red in the face and starts screaming and has to drop it. Then they lift it together and place it where it has to go. He asks her how she is getting on.

"Not s' bad," Barbro says, going to fetch another rock.

Martin shakes his head at Hans and asks whether women should be helping to build foundations in the first place.

Hans pretends not to hear, although he too has begun to wonder. But something has dawned on Maria: if the house is extended, then the reason for her wanting to sleep in the South Chamber is no longer there, the view she has, of her childhood across the water. But she can't bring herself to say anything until her husband has reached the sill along the top of the foundations and is about to start on the timber framework, what about the view, she asks, he has been grafting away for about a week.

Then she sees something she has never seen before, he sits down on the plinth and looks as if he is ready to throw everything in, both as a husband and as a man. Martin walks away in disgust muttering for Christ's sake. Maria cannot bring herself to console a man either, so she too walks across the yard, but there is nothing to stop Barbro sitting beside her brother and asking him what he is snivelling about, the way *he* used to ask *her*, when they were little. He waves her away, dries his sweat and without more ado resumes his work with the spade and adze, hacks off the layer of peat inside the foundation wall, loads it all onto the cart and runs it down to Bosom Acre, where it can be well employed to level the ground.

"Hva's wrong with tha nu?" Maria asks during dinner.

"Hva does tha think?" Hans says.

The next morning he rows to the main island and returns with the *færing* loaded to the gunwales with bags of cement, which he has bought on tick. He sets about carting in sand and starts concreting, a new wall on the inner side of the one that is already up, a concrete wall, then he cements a kind of floor on the rock base, it is uneven, but watertight. He nails boards to the timber sills and builds the wall a foot higher, as far as his cement allows. When the boards are removed what they have resembles a grey box of stone added on to the house, five by three metres and a good metre high.

The extension has become a rainwater tank.

Hans Barrøy hammers together some long boards, in a U-shape, and fixes them under both eaves, as gutters, then attaches two ducts which lead diagonally down and meet above the tank, in a funnel formation. He finds some planks and sets about making a lid. It looks like a floor, and is just as solid, they can sit and walk on it. Hans makes a hatch for it, hinged in such a way that it doesn't obstruct the buckets that will be lowered and raised.

Impressed, old Martin laughs.

As the weather is good the evening they finish fixing gutters to the barn roof too, they have supper sitting on the tank lid. One wet July later the tank is full. The water is clear, crystalline, unlike the dirty brown liquid the animals will now have all to themselves. After the next Lofoten season Hans wants to get a hand pump as well and install it in the kitchen. It is not the pump itself which is the challenge but the copper piping which has to run under the whole house and will presumably freeze during the winter. Ideally, the tank should have been on the north side of the house, up against the kitchen wall. They sleep in the North Chamber when it is too hot in Maria's preferred room or when the rain makes too much noise. Similarly they carry their eiderdowns to the South Chamber when it is too cold at the north end. The joys of life.

9

They and the inhabitants of other islands exchange breeding bulls and rams. If the Barrøy islanders have a ram it is kept apart from the ewes and lambs. It has an islet to itself, which is called Ramholm. It grazes there throughout most of the year eating grass and seaweed, and comes home for only a month around Christmas, when it services the ewes. When the time comes, Hans goes to get it, and Ingrid accompanies him.

Ingrid is afraid of the ram, it is vicious. But her father corners it on a headland with a large stick, grabs its fringe, turns it over, ties its legs together and drags it onto the boat while Ingrid looks on in trepidation. There is a lot of life in the ram. It is a mad, raging beast. With long, shaggy, unruly hair, salty crusts of sand and soil flapping around its hooves and a swaying thick black armour coat that stinks of sea and cowshed. When they arrive on Barrøy Hans puts a rope around its neck and it is so sore and docile after the crossing that Hans is able to lead it up to the barn without any further resistance. After it has done its duty they transport it back to Ramholm, or, on the rare occasion, to one of the other islets, where no sheep are grazing at the time.

All the islands have names. One of them is called Knuten. Once the ram tried to escape. It swam over to Knuten. When they discovered this they just let it stay there. Three days later it swam back. That taught him a lesson, Hans said. Ingrid thought it was frightening. If it's lonely why doesn't it swim to an island with sheep on? She also wonders if it might be blind. That would make it even more frightening. But even a blind ram can hear, can't it?

When the sun goes down in a sea of flames out there they can see the ram silhouetted against the red horizon, a tiny insect on a rocky raft afloat on the sea. And if the wind is in the right direction they can also hear it bellowing.

"He's cryen' out t' God," Barbro said.

It is the same for the ram as with other animals, it dies. But then it has to be buried. The ram is the only animal they don't eat.

10

They don't eat eider ducks either, but then the eider isn't a domestic bird, even though they build small stone houses for it, in order to collect the down, and for years they have had one nesting under the porch steps. So the cat has to be kept indoors for weeks. It doesn't like that because it is only allowed in Martin's room, where there are no curtains it can tear to shreds. The cat is called Bonken, it is a tom, because they can't have a cat that keeps having kittens, which Hans would have to kill, they say, but it is the same with cats as it is with all other animals on an island, how can they have young if there is only one of them?

In late spring, when the weather is so bad that it's not possible to do anything outside, Barbro and Maria set to work cleaning the down with their carding frame and comb. Down is the most valuable, mysterious material they handle. You can touch it and put it to your face and feel a distant, sacred warmth. You can compress it in your hand and it feels like nothing but air, and then open your palm and watch it expand into a grey cloud once more, as though nothing has happened.

When it is time to sell the down they pack it into canvas

sacks, attach a label to a cord and tie up the sack. On the label they write the year the down was collected, the name of the island and one kilo. A kilo of down is amazingly voluminous and unimaginably light. So even the high price it commands is ridiculously low. That is why they keep most of it for them-selves. This is Hans's idea. They use it in their own eiderdowns like the genteel folk in towns, or they store it in the driest loft above the cowshed, until prices pick up and they can sell it for twice as much as they get on the market in the summertime, or from Tommesen at the Trading Post, since the price of down is lowest when people want to sell and highest when only Hans wants to sell. He is the sole islander to have any success with this policy. This may be because the Barrøyers are slightly better off than others, since Hans receives a full catch share in Lofoten, but it might also be due to his family being more patient. Islanders need to be more patient than everyone else.

Barbro doesn't like carding down, her hands are not nimble enough, so from the summer when Ingrid turned four she had to pitch in and help her mother. Ingrid loves down, at first she just wants to play with it, and makes a mess on the tiny bench where they are sitting. But then she discovers that if you hold a ball of uncarded down in one hand and a ball of carded down in the other you cannot bear the thought of not cleaning it all, it would drive you mad if you didn't remove the small bits of twig and grass and shell, you would rather die than suffer that.

It is her mother who has taught her this. Telling her to sit still with her eyes closed and feel the two fistfuls of down, one carded and one uncarded, while she counts aloud, and she only gets to ten or eleven before she sees from her daughter's smile that she has realised what this is all about. Then she says, now you have learned something you will never forget.

From that day on Ingrid cards much faster than Barbro, who is thereby relieved of this drudgery and can be in the barn or the boat shed repairing fishing nets like a man.

11

Barbro can also *make* new fishing nets, cod nets and herring nets and flounder nets, she can even make trammel nets. This is how she spends the major part of the winter while Hans is in Lofoten. The nice thing about new nets is that they are clean and dry and don't stink, you can sit in the kitchen with floats and needles and sew, and sew, with the murmuring heat from the stove at your back, no matter how cold it is outside.

But Martin doesn't like it, having the kitchen full of work, fishing gear should be outside, in the open air or in the boat shed.

Cleaning and repairing nets in the freezing cold is the worst job in the world, it is the type of work that has ruined all the hands up and down the coast because it is the only kind that cannot be done with mittens on, Martin sees it as a luxury to be able to handle dry, new nets, unless of course it has to be done indoors in front of a stove full of glowing peat, it is not only unnecessary, it is stupid, and he doesn't need yet another reminder that his youngest daughter is the way she is.

Barbro couldn't care less what her father says.

Nor could any of the others. It must have happened only a

few years ago, although none of them can put a finger on exactly what it was that caused it, but from one day to the next, Martin stopped being the person who decided everything on the island, from then on it was Hans.

But if no-one else can remember, Martin can: it was the time when they found the Russian tree trunk and didn't know what to do with it. He and his son were in the process of levering it onto a skid with a crowbar, but when he applied his strength, his powers deserted him without warning, as fast as a steel rod being thrust into soft, wet ground. A short circuit in his brain. He had to sit down and get his breath back, gasping for air, while his son was left bearing all the weight.

From then on the tone was different.

The others noticed as well.

Even Ingrid has begun to develop bad habits. For example, she won't put up with being told not to do something by her grandfather, she goes to her mother who will often allow her to do whatever it is Martin wants to stop her doing. Maria sometimes sides with her father-in-law, according to her mood, as though she simply does not give a damn about whether he is there or about what he says.

Martin has accepted this. But he has become angry. When he was young, as a man is for many years, he was never angry, now he is all the time. No-one cares about that either. In the late spring nights the cat sleeps on his stomach in his small room. Through the thin wall they can hear him snoring and the cat purring. It is laughable. When the eider duck beneath the porch steps has finally hatched her eggs and guided the tiny fluff balls down the long path to the sea, the cat is let out again and sleeps for the rest of the year under the stove in the kitchen, unless he is out catching mice and fledglings.

Bonken, the cat, comes to a tragic end.

He was snatched by an eagle. It happened during the hay-making season. They heard screams, looked up from the drying racks and their rakes and saw a blurred ink blot beneath a sea eagle's immense wingspan. He was squirming and clawing and hissing and for a moment they thought he would succeed in breaking free. He did too. But it was only as he began to fall that they realised how high up he was. They saw him kick out his legs like a bat taking to the wing, and plummet into eternity, then for no apparent reason he suddenly pawed the air, perhaps because he was tired of falling and wanted to start running, but instead he flipped over and hit the rock face by the Lofoten boat shed, spine first.

It was too high, even for a cat, Hans said. And that became a catchphrase on the island, which he always returned to when something exceeded even an islander's powers.

Ingrid and Barbro buried Bonken at the far end of Rose Acre and placed some shells in the shape of a heart on his grave. Barbro sang a hymn. Ingrid cried. And a week or so later Hans brought home another cat. It was a female and was named Karnot, after a man Hans had gone to school with and who he thought looked like a cat, they called him Catman when he was small, too. Karnot was brown and as lovely as freshly made caramel pudding, graceful and cuddly, and was allowed to sleep on the kitchen table when the menfolk were out. At night she slept at the foot of Ingrid's bed. They called her a day cat as she slept just as long as and at the same times as humans. But Karnot also had to stay inside when the eider duck waddled over next summer to prepare its nest under the porch steps. The eider is a sacred animal.

12

Winter begins with a storm. They call it the First Winter Storm. There have been earlier storms, in August and September, for example, bringing sudden and merciless changes to their lives.

But as a rule these storms are short-lived. It is during one of them that the trees lose their leaves. As mentioned before, there are not many trees on the island but there are plenty of fruit bushes and dwarf birches and sallows – whose leaves in the course of late summer turn yellow, then brown and red at varying speeds – making the island, on some days in September, resemble a rainbow on earth. And so it looks until a sudden storm is unleashed upon them, sweeping the colours into the sea, transforming Barrøy into a whimpering, brown-furred animal, which it will remain until next spring, when it will no longer resemble a white-coated corpse beneath heaps of snow and slush, and the driving snow comes and goes, and comes once more, forming drifts, as though trying to imitate the sea on land. But they have experienced these storms many times before, they can even remember the last time, a year ago.

The First Winter Storm, on the other hand, is quite a different matter.

It is violent every single time and makes its entrance with a vengeance, they have never experienced anything like it, even though it also happened last year. This is the origin of the phrase "in living memory", they have simply forgotten how it was, since they have no choice but to ride the storm, this hell on earth, in the best way they can, and erase it from their memories as soon as possible.

Now they are in the midst of one such storm, it has raged with undiminished fury for more than a day and a night, with wispy flakes of snow swirling like tufts of wool above the island, rain as hard as hail and spring tides that do not ebb. Hans has been out three times to tie down things he didn't even consider it possible to tie down. He has seen one of his sheep being blown into the sea before he had time to lock the others in the boat shed, they haven't done the slaughtering yet and they have no room for all of them anywhere else, and inside he tethers them to the *færing* which he also ties down with its own mooring rope, it is unbelievable what men get into their heads when the First Winter Storm strikes.

He has also attached guy ropes to the new rainwater tank cover, a task which took him several hours. And he has to gather up the new roof gutters that are strewn all over the ground and place heavy rocks on top of them before he can crawl back home, by which time he is so drenched and his face so contorted that Ingrid can hardly recognise him.

She doesn't like these storms, the creaking of the house and the trumpet blasts from the chimney, the whole universe in turmoil, the wind that tears the breath out of her lungs when she goes to the barn with her mother, that drives the moisture from her eyes and sweeps her into walls and bowed trees, and forces the entire family to camp down in the kitchen and sitting room, and even there they don't get a wink of sleep. Martin too sits still when the winter storm ravages his island, with his woolly hat on his head and his great hands resting like empty, immovable shells on his knees. Unless he is holding them around Ingrid, who perambulates between him and the table and the oven and the pantry, and sits on the peat bin, dangling her feet, after which she goes back to Grandad and plays with his hands as if they were teddy bears.

The adults' faces are chiselled in stone. They whisper and knit their brows and make attempts to laugh but see through their own play-acting and revert to a more serious mood, the buildings on Barrøy have withstood everything so far, it is true, but that is no more than proof of the past: once there was a house in Karvika, there isn't any longer.

The sight of her father is the worst. Had Ingrid not known better she might have thought he was afraid, and he never is. Islanders are never afraid, if they were they wouldn't be able to live here, they would have to pack their goods and chattels and move and be like everyone else in the forests and valleys, it would be a catastrophe, islanders have a dark disposition, they are beset not with fear but solemnity.

This solemnity doesn't disperse until the head of the family has been outside once more and returns with blood on his face, remarking with a grin:

"Lovely weither out thar nu."

It takes them a while to realise that this is meant as a joke, and after they have wiped the blood off him and see that he has only a small cut on his chin, at which point he asks for a cup of coffee and says that th' old rowan has started t' lean t'east, they understand that the wind, once again, has changed direction from the terrible south-west to the west, which is the first sign that another hurricane is about to subside into an ordinary storm, and then turn into a northerly and drop to a moderate gale before finally abating enough for them to be able to carry water to the cowshed without arriving with empty buckets. Barbro and Maria can now manage to get them to the animals almost half-full, while Hans stands in the kitchen musing and fiddling with the cut on his chin; suddenly, however, he is struck by a sudden thought and tells Ingrid to go out with him to look at the sea, so that she will learn not to fear it, now, while it is at its most tempestuous, at its most instructive.

He doesn't know why this idea occurs to him.

She doesn't, either. But he puts on her coat, Martin is shaking his head, and ties a rope around her waist. They go out, the raging firmament above them, drag themselves southwards, wade against the current in a river of wind and water, struggle over three stone walls and crouch down behind one to catch their breath, clamber over another, Ingrid's father laughing at every obstacle, she has to hold both hands in front of her face to breathe, up to the knoll behind the Russian tree trunk, which constitutes the last bastion against the roar that comes to meet them – foaming walls of water towering up in the black night and crashing down towards them, smashing against rock and beach and stone, causing sand and shell and ice to lash at them, this is something no-one can face, or comprehend, or remember, the trumpets of doom, all you can do is rid it from your mind.

"It won't hurt tha," her father screams in her ear.

But she doesn't hear. Neither of them hears. He screams that she has to feel with her body that the island is immovable, even though it trembles and both the heavens and the sea are in tumult, an island can never go under, although it may quake, it is rock solid and eternal, it is *fixed* to the earth itself. Yes, at this moment it is almost a religious belief he wants to share with his daughter, since he doesn't have a son, and with every day that passes he becomes more and more convinced that he will never have one and he will have to content himself with a daughter and teach her the basic principle that an island can never founder, never.

Later, Ingrid will reflect on how strange this evening was, something I'll never forget, she will say, but this is long after the storm has passed, and only that which is unshakeable remains, the question of whether an island is more than a grain of sand. These thoughts are prompted not by her father but by her mother, who, after they have struggled home again, receives them with a barrage of reproach, complaining that she cannot even go to the cowshed without this idiot of a husband endangering the life of her daughter, if he gets any more of these crazy ideas, A'll divorce tha an' bi gone.

It is not the first time such words have been uttered in this plain-speaking household, they have nerves of steel, but it is the first time Ingrid has understood their implications: you *can* leave an island.

She starts crying, and it is a while before Maria realises that it is not the storm but her own words that have upset Ingrid, there is nothing to them, they are only sound and fury. But she can't bring herself to say so, of course they are never going to leave Barrøy, it is an impossible idea, especially now that the First Winter Storm is in its death throes, beyond the creaking walls, in these situations people are not themselves and cannot see that once you settle on an island, you never leave, an island holds on to what it has with all its might and main.

13

In the following days they walk along the beaches in the south of the island, Hans Barrøy with a pitchfork, Martin with a boathook and the others each carrying a rake. They rummage through the piles of seaweed the storm has thrown up, huge brown swathes over the fields and stone walls, entwined like tough, slippery rope, they tear them apart and find bits of wood and line tubs and bailers and a mysterious tea chest with a scorpion on the lid, a wall clock without any works and a swollen book with the print gone, objects that they hold up and show each other with cries of wonderment, whereafter they carry them up on land and place them in the cart hitched to the stoop-necked horse which stands there chewing, then lies down because it can't be bothered to stand any longer, it lies there between the shafts of the cart like an ox.

The horse.

It is not a young horse. It wasn't when it arrived either. It came by boat, the biggest ship Ingrid has seen, and was hoisted ashore in a strap by a crane and deposited on the rocky ground by the Lofoten boat shed, where one day they are going to build a quay. At that time the horse was wild and had an evil look, it showed the whites of its eyes and kicked and whinnied and bit. All they could do was cut it loose and let it run free until it came to its senses. It was supposed to be a quiet horse, it certainly was when it had stood peacefully in a meadow at the Trading Post, where in truth it had had its day. That was why Hans got it so cheap. For a song.

But it was amusing to watch this new islander. It galloped like a lunatic across the island, pulled up suddenly when it met the sea to the east and charged off south until it met more sea and turned in its tracks again and ran north and tossed its head and gave it everything it had, the old nag, until once more it met a wall of sea and carried on and on like this until it had visited so many nooks and crannies of its new home that it was forced to realise it was on an island which it, too, would never leave.

But it wasn't a good-natured horse.

It was in the cowshed with the other animals, but had to be given its own trough and a partition between it and the cows because it bit and kicked, and only Hans could manage it, at first by dint of a stick and his boot. But gradually they came to a kind of agreement, whereby the horse could basically do what it wished, and there was no real problem with that, so long as it pulled the cartfuls of hay and peat and the mower, which they could only use on the four flattest meadows, and in addition a simple plough that Hans had been given at no extra cost, to make the potato plot bigger and easier to work, yes, on these conditions Hans could turn a blind eye to it lying down and sleeping a lot and tossing its head wildly which meant that his daughter couldn't ride it, not even when he was holding the bridle. But it didn't have a name.

Everything on the island that was wild had a name.

Bird's-foot trefoil, clover, Aaron's rod, stork's beak, buttercup, heath-spotted orchid, meadowsweet, angelica, harebell, foxglove, saxifrage, mayweed and sorrel. Herring gull, auk, cormorant, guillemot, puffin, heron, sandpiper, curlew, wheatear and the white wagtail. Vole and sea urchin, razor clam, giant's kettle and North Wind Ridge, crowberry, calluna, rhubarb, nettle and whooper swans which greet two seasons with mournful trumpet fanfares . . . And everything that was tame had two names, cows, sheep, cats and even the pig, which they had for only six months, but not the horse, and that is a double oddity as it is both a domestic animal yet so unlike all the others of the same kind, but that is how it is with this animal, it is like nothing else.

Now the cart is full and Hans pokes the horse in the ribs with the tip of his boot and brings it to its feet, clicks his tongue and walks beside it up through the Acres to the boat shed in the north, where he gives it some dry hay in a canvas sack, which he ties to the door, so that the beast doesn't take it and run away.

They unload all the items the storm has brought to the shores, sort through them, it is mostly wood, which is sawn up and stacked, but there are also twenty-eight glass floats, which Martin will see to, five markers with or without buoys, one with sixty yards of rope in tow, which Hans rolls up and hangs on a hook in the boat shed. Four whole net pegs, with line, five fish boxes, some of which are taken to the Lofoten shed, three line tubs, one missing a single stave, to be repaired by Martin, enough poles to make half a drying rack, a ship's hold cover that it requires two of them to lift, six sea boots, all left feet and only one that can't be used because someone has cut off the heel, or else it has been bitten off.

And a carnival mask.

Hans holds it up in front of his face to frighten Ingrid, but removes it again quickly because it stinks and has to be washed in hot water.

It is a devil's mask, with red lightning for eyebrows and a black moustache and empty eye holes, a toothless mouth and high white cheekbones with red whirls which make it look both dangerous and genial. A stupid, vacuous face. It will probably be fine if they can get the slime and seaweed and barnacles off – a hue of its own, like crackled varnish, giving it an unusual depth – enough to secure it a place on the wall in the parlour where it will hang for an age before being discovered by a stranger to the house, who offers a high price for it. He says that of course it isn't worth as much as he is offering, but a mask hanging here, a foreign body in a simple house on a remote island, that makes it especially interesting, it has to be a sign of something, the stranger says, without giving any further explanation.

But this kind of talk makes the islanders sceptical, so they don't sell it, this mask can stay on the parlour wall, now they also know it is French, it costs them nothing to hang on to it, they believe in God, not in signs.

After the storm they also find five tarred posts, all with drill holes, many of the bolts are intact, all of them new-looking. This makes them suspect they are debris from the same quay. So someone has a lost a whole quay in this storm, a very *new* quay. And this someone can't be far away, perhaps it is even folk they know on one of the islands to the south, so Hans and Martin pick up the posts and put them with the others they have collected for constructing what will one day be their own quay, but in a separate pile. They tell each other that such precious timber should be exempt from the rule that after storms finders are keepers, this is almost like finding a boat adrift, with a number and name, and that belongs to the owner, until further notice. But they have a lot of material now, so even if the posts can't be used straight away, the idea has moved a step closer, the idea that they cannot live here without a quay.

14

In February the sea is sometimes a turquoise mirror. Snow-covered Barrøy resembles a cloud in the sky. It is the frost that makes the sea green, and clearer, and calm and viscous, like jelly. Then it can completely congeal with a translucent film on the surface and change from one state to another. The island has acquired a rim of ice, which also surrounds the closest islets, it has increased in size.

Ingrid stands in woollen *lugg* boots on a floor of glass midway between the island and Moltholmen and beneath her she can see seaweed and fish and shells in a summer landscape. Sea urchins and starfish and black rocks in white sand and fish darting through a swaying forest of kelp, the ice is a magnifying glass, as clear as air, she is floating on the water and six years old, it is impossible not to walk on the ice once it has formed.

She has watched it become thicker and safer, she has smashed a hole in it with a stone, she has stolen one of her father's axes and chopped at it, she has wriggled her way yard after yard from the shore, and whatever can't be smashed can be walked on.

Now she is walking in her sleep over to Moltholmen, which

also resembles a cloud in the sky, she is sitting in the snow, taking deep breaths, she discovers it is no more dangerous on ice than on land. She ventures out onto the ice again and teeters back, there isn't a sound in the world, no wind, no birds, not even the sea.

She takes a run-up and slides, runs and throws herself onto her stomach and slides back towards the island and she is twenty or so yards from land when a voice cuts through the silence. It is her mother, who has seen her from the yard and comes racing towards her gesticulating wildly with her mouth agape, over wall and crag, powdery snow puffing up around her feet.

But then she stops on the beach, as if she has met a barrier, and starts running to and fro, obstructed by a hindrance that isn't there. That makes Ingrid laugh. She takes another run-up and slides, her mother screams no, no, continuing to run back and forth behind the invisible barrier until something in her eyes snaps and she takes a first step onto the ice, her arms outstretched like a tightrope walker, holding her breath and biting her lip, her fury doesn't relent until she has grabbed her daughter, sure in the knowledge that both of them are safe.

Maria stiffens and stands looking around, she can't believe it, they are floating.

"Come on," she says.

They take a few sliding steps, then a run-up, and slide the last few yards to the shore laughing and gasping for breath. But Ingrid pulls herself free and goes back on the ice. Maria screams no, no, again, but follows her. They hold hands and slide along the shore to the north, into coves and round promontories, between tiny skerries and islets until they hear a voice and spot Barbro walking from the boat shed with her chair, staring at them, horror-stricken. They return to the shore and drag her onto the ice, sit her down on the chair and spin her round, slide her past the northern tip of the island, but don't go ashore here either because Barbro has acquired a taste for it now too, they keep whirling her round, she screams and dribbles, round Ytterneset and as far as the ruins in Karvika.

There they walk up into the snow and carry the chair home. Barbro is not allowed to take it outside, not even when she goes to the boat shed to mend nets.

The only person not to go on the ice is Martin. He stays indoors refusing to believe there is any ice, even though they insist, there has never been ice here before, the tides make it impossible, no matter how hard the frost or how great the silence. He has no intention of going to look either. But when his son returns home safe and sound from Lofoten once again, at about the same time as the oystercatchers come back, and Hans asks if there is any-thing new, Martin tells him that they had ice here this winter, all around the island, it was only there for a few hours, but it was so thick that they could walk on it, until a gale broke it up and washed it ashore, where it lay like a rampart of broken glass for several weeks until it melted, that was at the end of March.

The son asks if he has completely lost his mind. And old Martin regrets having told him.

15

Two days into the New Year they see lights in the winter darkness. Uncle Erling's boat appears out of the night and bobs up and down off the sheer rock face, known as the Hammer, until the islanders have collected themselves. It doesn't take long. They have been waiting for this moment.

If the weather is good Hans places a wobbly plank between the Hammer and the railing on the boat and, like a circus performer, carries on board ten line tubs, three crates of floats, twelve sea markers, rigging and a heavy Lofoten chest, which one of the hired hands has to help him with, rugs and barrels of sour milk and oilskins, while Uncle Erling hangs out of the wheelhouse window inspecting the weather and chatting to their father, Martin, who is standing on the brow of the rock with his hands in his pockets, as though they had last seen each other yesterday whereas in fact it was eight months ago, in May, when Hans was delivered to this same place after the previous season in Lofoten. But nothing has happened since, no-one has died and no-one has been born, and our Helga says hello by the way.

If the weather is bad Hans also puts out this plank, but it

takes him much, much longer to get the fishing equipment on board. Uncle Erling hangs out of the wheelhouse then too, and yells the same phrases, which are borne on the wind before reaching land, while manoeuvring the heaving boat with his left hand so that it stays just clear of the rock face every time Ingrid thinks, this is it, there is going to be a disaster, and closes her eyes.

Martin still doesn't lend a hand.

He stands there, the skipper of this island, leaving his younger son to struggle with the gear while he chats with his older son in the wheelhouse about something in exactly the same way he would do if there were no wind.

Maria and Barbro are also present, their arms folded over their chests, leaning against the wind, their headscarves flapping like pennants. Maria sometimes shouts an amusing remark over to Uncle Erling, who grins and answers something Ingrid can't catch, but which Maria laughs at and Martin ignores. Barbro would like to help her brother with the tubs, but she knows they don't want women on a sea-going vessel. For safety's sake, they don't have waffles on board or brown cheese either, and they never whistle, whistle at sea and you are as good as done for, whether you believe in God or fate, it makes no difference.

Ingrid is freezing cold, frozen to the marrow, she always is when she stands here watching her father leave. It is the second day of the year, the saddest of all three hundred and sixty-five, and it is brought to a close by the sight of the swaying aft lantern which recedes into the roaring night like a burning ember up a chimney stack.

Then the gravity takes hold of them.

Not the gravity of the storm, but the year's and the island's slow lessons in loneliness. Suddenly there are fewer of them, they walk around and have lost the head of the island. They talk in hushed voices or are silent, short-tempered and impatient. Furthermore, Lofoten is a place you don't necessarily return from unscathed, you are dicing with death, where more than two hundred men lose their lives every winter, which they don't say aloud, they only hint at it. Neither are there any cemeteries on earth with more graveless crosses than those Our Lord holds His hand over along this coast.

And so the days pass, in January.

Along with three more months. Of frost and snowdrifts and Old Nick.

Until, strangely enough, this gravity is illuminated with new hope. It rises with the sun in the black sky. First, like a bruised eye at the beginning of January, then bloodier and bloodier through February, until it finally lights up in the sky like the crater it is to be; they have sent a man on a wing and a prayer into the seething darkness, now they are hoping to get him back alive, perhaps even with his pockets full of money, this after all is what gives the island hope, their head of family has his own fishing gear and a full catch share.

They also receive word from him, one letter.

Letters like this are delivered by Thomas from the

neighbouring island of Stangholmen, or by somebody sent from Havstein, where the men stay at home in the winter and fish local waters, they normally arrive one fine day at Easter.

But this letter is short.

And it isn't written the way they clearly remember their husband and brother and son and father used to speak, it is couched in ornate, biblical language, as though it has been penned by a stranger. They feel he has moved even further away from them, to such a degree that they would actually have preferred to be without the whole epistle. Maria says so too, though now at least they know he is safe and sound, for the time being anyway, the fishing has been as it always has been, they have been informed about his forced time ashore and a man who steams cod liver and is also a cobbler and has sewn Hans a new pair of hobnail boots, so he won't freeze in his old ones, and that is something, yes, it is indeed, upon mature reflection.

Then at last he comes back home, as his own lean self, looking three years older with half-crazed eyes, from both an urge to be active and a lack of sleep, as though he can't make up his mind whether to start on this quay they need straight away or simply go to bed, for ever.

They are strange days, these days after the homecoming, the return of a father and a husband and a brother and a son. It is also the end of April now and the light has driven away the darkness for good, there is not even any night, only morning, the lambs have appeared with the first green shoots of grass and the eider duck has waddled ashore. The traveller can be content that everything is as it is and has been because it is always the person who has been away who gains the greatest pleasure from knowing time stands still.

There is laughter in the North Chamber in the morning, after which Ingrid's parents come down to the kitchen, where there is an aroma of coffee again, after a break of four months, women don't drink coffee alone, and Martin is saving up, he says. Hans tells stories from his stay up north, anecdotes that have to be explained and embellished. He has to keep pointing out how much Ingrid has grown, she is almost too big to sit on his lap now, she sits there anyway and will be sitting there for a few years yet. It is all eggs and spring farming and eider down and the peaceful summer months, when they work round the clock, and then comes autumn, when the quay becomes a reality, not a quay of tarred posts as planned but one built of rock, this is because everything is not as it should be in Ingrid's happy childhood after all, there is unrest in the world, it is ablaze.

16

They say that two things in life are inescapable, poverty and war. And this winter has not only been hard, but also mean, with poor catches. But today, in June, Hans is at the Trading Post, where he hears a foreign language, it is Swedish. Five men, unknown to him, are standing in a circle around Tommesen, the owner, and one of them is speaking Swedish. The others say nothing. But they are Swedish, too.

In the salting room Hans hears that the situation in Sweden is bad because of the war, the five men outside are bricklayers and willing to work for only their board and lodging, now they are going to lay the plinth of Tommesen's new barn, and after that the foundations for the new stockfish store.

Hans has actually come to the Post to buy salt and some herring barrels, but now he buys bolts, boards and six tarred posts, together with one hundred and sixty running metres of planking, two by five inches, for money of which he has only half. He has to have the materials delivered. He can't afford this either, but he doesn't give a damn.

When he gets back to the island he talks to Maria in private and the following day sets about digging post holes on the shore, without consulting Martin. Not on the far side of the Lofoten Hammer. The posts are driven down in the cove on this side of it. This is the beginning of a boat shed, far too big, which is to stand on stakes so that it can be entered from the land on what resembles a gently sloping barn bridge, and there will be a large door in the west-facing wall, a platform jutting out with some steps down to the shore, so that at high tide small boats can moor. But this is only half of the dream, in the old man's view, as if his son hasn't got the nerve to go for the whole thing, or the money, as usual?

It rains all June. Night and day. May has been too dry, but now the tank is filled again, the ponds, too, and the rock pools which the animals drink from. The trenches in the bog, where they have excavated peat in recent years, are filled to over their banks and become square, brown lakes, they have to take care the animals don't fall in.

And there is no haymaking this year.

But in the middle of July a steady easterly wind sets in, the weather clears up and everything dries out, the marsh-brown lakes subside, leaving a black, cracked crust. They manage to save half of the hay. Before it starts to rain again, non-stop. And the rest of the hay is lost. But at the beginning of September the new boathouse is finished. They don't fill it with the fishing gear and tools they have had lying outdoors: there are five bunk beds there, with fresh straw and blankets, a table in front of the window, two chairs and a bench.

Three days later the Trading Post cargo boat arrives with five Swedish workmen on board. They have walked all the way from their own country, through forests and over mountains, it has taken three weeks, each of them carrying a rucksack full of provisions and tools, during the summer they worked at the Trading Post, now they are here, and they are good.

They blast the rocks they need from the Hammer and build, employing the same technique Hans used when he built the rainwater tank. After only a week they are above the high-water mark and can work in dry clothes, it has been a fine, clear autumn with colours which last and a *föhn* that sweeps over man and beast like moist breath. During this Indian summer they also salvage some of the lost hay, and the whole family spends a good week on the islets scything, they row the hay home every evening and dry it on the slopes to the south of the yard, then carry it straight to the barn, it is green, but dry.

And the Swedes are another metre higher.

But they eat an awful lot. Bread with rhubarb jam, which Maria and Barbro bake and boil. On Sundays they are also given butter and coffee. And every day Maria boils fish and serves up the last of their old potatoes, she empties the cellar and for the first time since she arrived on the island she seizes the opportunity to give it a proper cleaning. She washes and scrubs and finds three mouse holes, which Hans seals with cement. They repair a frost-damaged outer wall with peat, and they put in new stalls on the lower floor of the barn, then the potato harvest begins. They dig them up while the hard-working Swedes toil their way another metre upwards. Now the only question is whether the platform should be of wood or stone.

Hans has used all the materials he has on the boathouse where the guests sleep, a little more in fact, the floor of the quay will have to be stone too.

It is a masterpiece. He has tears in his eyes the day he can walk on the quay, a rock-solid mosaic of red granite in all Barrøy's hues and shades, a church floor grouted with white shell sand. On the seaward side, eight bolted posts lead down into the sea, three of them rising about a metre above the quay so the boats will have something to moor to. They can accommodate a steamship. And they can hold it in place with two lines, a forward and aft spring. But now the proud Lofoten boat shed has become so pitifully small, it looks like an outside toilet, badly positioned and a mottled grey. Hans already has new plans in place for next year.

It has been strange having foreigners on the island. After all, the population has doubled. And the very first week they have to keep Barbro away from the building site.

"A want t' fuck," she shouts, and Maria has to cover Ingrid's ears. Her sister-in-law "isn't all thar".

Barbro shouts some other things that Ingrid shouldn't hear. But Ingrid doesn't like her ears being covered, and in the end she realises what it is all about, Barbro tells her, and at the same time reveals that one of the Swedes is called Lars Klemet. He is no more than twenty and the only one of them who speaks in a way she can understand. Ingrid likes Lars Klemet, he is funny and jokes and talks to her when he is not working, and he can sing. Barbro can, too. She takes her chair to the Hammer and sits there like a vigilant queen watching the workers building, men doing their work, slim, naked bodies glistening with sweat and salt and getting browner and browner in the long late summer, sinews and muscles at play beneath the skin of a man at the peak of his powers. She bakes and takes them fresh bread and a new pot of jam, if there is one thing they have enough of, it is rhubarb. Lars Klemet is moreover the only one who washes in the sea, so he smells more of salt water and seaweed than horse, and also says that he has never had better food and pinches Barbro's buttocks when nobody is watching, but how big is the island?

It is a little under a kilometre from north to south, and half a kilometre from east to west, it has lots of crags and small grassy hollows and dells, deep coves cut into its coast and there are long rugged headlands and three white beaches. And even though on a normal day they can stand in the yard and keep an eye on the sheep, they are not so easy to spot when they are lying down in the long grass, the same goes for people, even an island has its secrets.

Another factor is that Maria and Hans, and not least Martin, gradually lose interest in what Barbro gets up to, there is the haymaking and hay-drying to see to.

When the Swedes finally leave – the islanders shake all of them by the hand, including Ingrid – they are each given a small sum of money in addition to the board and lodging they have received, it has cost Hans everything he has, and more, but he knows what he has in return, a quay of stone that will last forever, so he can't send the workmen away without giving them more than they ask for. He should have given them what they deserve, but he doesn't have that, so the result is a compromise, which is to the satisfaction of both parties. They leave in rain, it sets in at the beginning of October and stays, and even though the people on the island heave a sigh of relief at being back to the number they usually are, they think it is sad. Having visitors has its advantages. When they leave, the islanders are left with only themselves and feel this might not be enough. Visitors create a loss. They make it clear to the islanders that they lack something, presumably they did so before their guests arrived, and will continue to do so.

17

Háns has a telescope. What is special about it is that he just *has* it, somewhere, and never uses it. He doesn't even remember where it came from. But now they are moving tackle and equipment from the jam-packed boat shed to the Swedes' boathouse. He finds a roll of oiled canvas and stands with it in his hands, wondering. It has been in his possession for as long as he can remember. He unrolls the canvas and thinks, this is the telescope, yes . . .

It is a telescope that can magnify forty times, a black lacquer- and leather-looking German model with four brass rings and an eyepiece, which is also made of brass, and a screw to adjust the focus.

He shows it to his father.

Martin says the same, yes, that's the telescope.

To the question of where it came from, however, he can give no more precise an answer than when they discuss the ruins in Karvika, he must have inherited it from his father, who was both a ship's pilot and reserve lighthouse man, when he wasn't a fisherman, that is, the telescope looks as if it would be at home on a sailing ship.

Hans takes it outside into the clear autumn light and inspects it more carefully, wondering why he never played with it as a child. Then he remembers. He wasn't allowed to. He mentions this to his father. Martin smiles and says he wasn't allowed to play with it either, his father didn't let him.

Hans sets it up on a sheet of slate they have placed on three stones outside the boathouse as a work table, squats down and focuses. He can see the mountains over on the mainland as clearly as if he were standing at the foot of them, they are already covered with the first snow, it glitters. But he can't see the coast, where he knows there are houses. The buildings have disappeared, behind the sea, due to the curvature of the earth.

Martin, too, takes a peek at the footless mountains.

They smile.

Hans trains the telescope on the main island, sees the church, the Trading Post, the rectory and the houses, one by one, mumbling that is where Konrad lives, that's Olav's place . . . He can see who has curtains in the windows and who has painted his house. But then he straightens up, feeling that he has encroached upon property where he has no business to be.

He hands the telescope to his father. Martin takes up position and it is not long either before he looks away. Hans has an inkling that they are of the same mind, perhaps they don't need this telescope. They take a pair of binoculars with them to Lofoten, they don't use them either, as everything they can see through them vanishes as soon as they stop looking.

But this telescope is heavy and solid, industrial workmanship of the highest quality, and must be worth a lot of money. Offhand, Hans can't think of anything else he owns which might be just as valuable, the sextant maybe, or the compass in Erling's ship, which is also an heirloom.

Anything else?

What does he actually have of any value?

He goes back to the house with the telescope and asks Maria to go up to the South Chamber with him. He sets it up on the windowsill and tells her to look across at Buøy, her childhood island home. She kneels on the bed, catches sight of her house and gives a start. He asks her what she can see. She says she is not sure, closes one eye again and concentrates. He lies down on the bed and looks up at her. She says she thinks she can see people. He can tell by her facial expression that she is bemused, as if she has tasted something and can't decide whether she likes it or not.

"Let me have a look," he says.

He can see the buildings, and count them, eighteen, including all the outhouses and the boat sheds. A boat moored by a jetty, it slowly sinks until only the top of the mast is visible, then rises just as slowly again. It is the swell that makes it disappear, and the swell that brings it back into view. But he can't see any people, though there is something, it might be sheep, or a horse, an autumn-ploughed field . . .

Maria takes the telescope from him again.

He lies back down with his arms behind his head and tells

her they have no money. She removes her eye from the telescope and stares at him. He repeats himself, and this time he doesn't look at her. She says she already knew, in a tone that suggests she wasn't happy about what she knew. And both of them have lost interest in the telescope.

She asks him why he is telling her this now. He says he doesn't know.

"Is it serious?" she asks. He doesn't answer. She asks how serious it is. He is sorry he mentioned the matter. Something happens in her eyes. She strikes him with the telescope, across the stomach. He asks if she intends to kill him. She says yes, brandishing the telescope once more. He grips her hands, feels an urge to tear off her clothes and put a smile on her face, in the middle of the day, in working hours, in broad daylight. Instead he gets to his feet and ignores what she screams at him, he knows what she is screaming, and goes downstairs and into the yard, where his father and Ingrid stand looking at him.

"Hva tha gawpen' at?"

Martin looks as though he has been caught red-handed, turns and walks down to the boat shed, his arms dangling by his sides. Hans stands watching him, the telescope in his hands, wondering whether to follow.

Ingrid asks him what it is. He says it is a telescope. She asks what *that* is.

Look, he says, walking over to the barn bridge, where he points it at a tuft of grass, and shows her. She looks into the eyepiece and recoils. That laugh of hers. It hasn't always been a joy to hear. She has another look, at the houses on Stanghol-men, and her smile remains until he says that's enough and takes the telescope with him down to the boat shed. He and his father stare at each other as if they have some unsorted business.

Not for long.

Martin picks up a fish crate containing coils of haddock lines and bait trays and lumbers off towards the new boathouse. Hans rolls up the telescope in the canvas, then follows him and places it on one of the top shelves, where it can stay until the next time it is found by someone who says, yes, that's the telescope, Hans muses that there must be a reason for the eye not seeing further than it does, that this might be an advantage for both the eye and the object it observes, now at any rate he has forgotten what he didn't want to think about, money, the most depressing link they have to the mainland.

18

I ngrid could hear from the noises in the kitchen alone that something was not as it should be. A sound was missing, the sound of Barbro.

What was more, her mother's voice was too loud and it fell silent too abruptly when Ingrid came down the stairs. Outside it was wintry, dark, no wind. In a few hours the sky would be lighter, later in the day they might perhaps catch a glimpse of red sun in the south. But Barbro wasn't there. She and the *færing* had disappeared, a search hadn't been necessary, the footsteps led in only one direction, through the new snow to the boat shed and not only that, both doors were wide open. She hadn't taken the sail, she had rowed, and on the sea they could see nothing.

They had several boats, a big and a small rowing boat, and another *færing*, a Binsdal. But none of them had been put into the water.

"Hvar's Barbro?" Ingrid asked.

"She's gone," her mother said.

The day passed without any more being said. Not even Grandfather's hands were as they usually were. His face was grey. At bedtime, Ingrid was allowed to sleep in her father's bed, as she used to do when he was in Lofoten. Maria said they would have to give the sheep more birch twigs in the coming days, it took them longer to eat, the hay was getting short, she was thinking about the cows and the horse. She also said the frost would hopefully relent, then they could let the animals go down to the beach, perhaps there would be milder weather and rain soon so that they could graze on some old grass.

Ingrid asked if she could knit in bed.

Maria asked if it wasn't too cold.

Not if she had an eiderdown over her shoulders.

Her mother lay beside her, explaining and showing her how to do it until she dropped off. Then Ingrid put down her knitting and fell asleep as well. When she woke up she saw that her mother was still asleep. So was the cat. From the pale light through the windowpanes she realised they had overslept. This was a new experience for her.

She got up and went down to the cold kitchen, put wood chippings and kindling in the stove and then peat, the way Barbro had taught her, Barbro had been in charge of the stove. Now Ingrid was. She saw that the peat bin was empty and took it out with her to the shed which was up against the north wall of the barn. It was cold. She kicked away the snow, opened the door on its creaking hinges and filled the bin, decided it was too heavy and took out half of the peat turfs, closed the door and returned to the house. By then her hands were frozen. She held them over the stove until they became red and began to tingle.

Then she went to her grandfather's room and saw that he was asleep too. She shook him. He got up as if from a bad dream.

"What th' devil," he said when he saw the grey light behind the frosted window panes. "Is that th' time!"

Then he went back to sleep.

Also the next morning. The adults overslept the next morning too. As though they had become lazy or were recuperating after a long period of strain. Or as though Barbro had been the clock in the house, the timekeeper, which had now stopped. But Ingrid got up, lit the fire and fetched peat. On the third day she heard her mother and grandfather arguing in the barn, where he hardly ever set foot. The argument was about the *færing*, they were angry with Barbro, who had taken the best boat when there were three others.

But there was something else that gave Ingrid a lead as she stood listening to them: they didn't appear surprised that Barbro had gone missing, even the most incomprehensible events can be anticipated, and consequently accepted. It was then she realised that Barbro was dead.

That night too she was allowed to knit in her father's bed. The yarn was sticky and smelled of lanolin, it was rust red and yellow and made her fingers soft and strong, she could bend them backwards until they cracked, she did that to hold back her tears. Maria told her to stop it. Then she said she could feel from the weather that the frost was soon going to break, and Ingrid, who was so good at knitting, she could make nets, cod nets, too, couldn't she?

"Mebbe," Ingrid said, Barbro had begun to teach her, she had made a small square of thick seine netting, in which they used to carry firewood, a bag, a net basket, which she also used to collect eggs. But it wasn't necessary, she said as every corner of her body grew warm, for they had enough nets, Barbro had done nothing else all winter, and now, soon, she would be back.

"No," her mother said. "She won't bi comen' agin."

"Yes, she will," Ingrid said.

19

The frost became more severe, north-easterly gales blew up, which made it feel even colder. Ingrid and her mother moved into the South Chamber above Martin's room. He stoked his private stove furiously down below, and they had the hatch in the floor open, so the heat rose. When her mother slept Ingrid could hear that her grandfather was also asleep, as though they were in the same room.

Martin couldn't do any fishing in this frost. They ate pollack and salted herring and potatoes and bread and jam. They ran out of thin birch twigs, but Martin didn't want to beachcomb for kelp to make fodder, it was too cold, they should have done it before, now it was too late, the sheep would have to go down to the beach.

Ingrid and Maria herded them there. But bundles of rattling ice began to hang from the animals' legs, which made them kick out and roll around until they were covered in an icy coat of mail, they became heavier and heavier and began to stagger under the weight. Ingrid could see that her mother was afraid. They drove them back home, had to drag several of them, and the ice on their wool didn't melt until they had been in the barn for more than a day. During that time they were given the hay the cows should have had and the seaweed Maria and Ingrid managed to rake up with a grapnel and pull home on a sled to boil up and make fodder. Martin didn't take part in this either, he stayed in bed grieving the loss of a daughter. The sheep were also given the little cod liver they had, pollack cooked to death and all the leftovers, they had begun to tremble and go dizzy.

Then Martin got up after all, donned as many clothes as he could squeeze into, pushed out the smaller rowing boat and set a string of gill nets in the water off the new boathouse. But the nets became sheets of ice as soon as he tried to pull them in. He had to leave them, night after night, picked off the fish as best he could every day, but after two weeks they were so full of seaweed and algae that they weren't catching fish anymore and all he could do was let them stay there, these were Barbro's newest nets.

But they had fresh fish again and crispbread, there were livers in the fish, and they had potatoes. Now, though, it was vital they refrain from going into the cellar, so they didn't let the frozen air in there too. They shovelled even more snow on top of it and stored potatoes in fish crates on the parlour floor, enough potatoes for a week at a time. They baked potato cakes on the kitchen stove, which usually they did only before Christmas. The house smelled of Christmas. Then the frost broke. Last year the winter had been so cold that a band of ice had encircled the island. This year it was much colder because of the wind.

20

Ingrid was the first to see the boat. She was standing up to her knees in wet snow on the headland by the boat shed and her fingers were no longer cold, not even when she formed snowballs to throw at the seagulls which thought they were food and swooped down and fought for them. On her head she had only one headscarf; in the frost she wore three and one in front of her face. Now she took it off and waved it, and for the first time this year she felt the wind in her hair, the winter was over.

It wasn't one boat but two, and the second one was being towed. In the first sat four black-clad oarsmen and three other people, in the other there was no-one, it was Barrøy's *færing*, which had gone missing with Barbro.

Ingrid recognised it by the colours along the side and ran up to the house to tell her mother. But Maria had seen them and was already on her way, Martin shuffled over as well, from the new boathouse, so they were all standing on the shore as the iron keel of the first boat hit land.

In the prow sat the priest's wife and another woman, whom at first Maria didn't recognise. In the stern behind the oarsmen sat Barbro, wearing unfamiliar clothes. She stood up and stepped over the oars, laid a hand on the priest's wife's shoulder, then came ashore and walked up towards the houses without saying a word. They stood watching her until she was inside and had closed the door behind her. Ingrid ran after her.

Karen Louise Malmberget said that Barbro didn't want to stay with her anymore, she had done her utmost to keep her, but it was no good, she cried and wanted to come back to Barrøy, but they hadn't been able to travel before because of the wind and frost.

Then she put both hands to her mouth when she realised that Barbro had not merely left the island but fled, and that the islanders thought they had lost her. At which point Karen Louise stood looking around, just as her husband had done an eternity ago, stared across at the buildings on the main island, where she herself came from, but which she had never seen before, and she said:

"How nice it is here."

It was such a meaningless statement that Martin said "Christ Almighty" and gave a surly "no" in answer to the oarsmen who asked if they could help him to put away the *færing*. He went into the boat shed and fetched two trestles, told them to pull the boat up onto the rollers, then lumbered up to the house as well. But that was for the best, for now Maria had recognised the other woman, her name was Elise Havstein, they had gone to school together.

They shook hands and smiled.

It was a stiff reunion. Elise Havstein was wearing clothes

she obviously hadn't sewn herself and was a midwife with a white scarf around her neck, which made her look like a nun, and Barbro was with child, she was due in the course of the summer, Karen Louise had brought her with her to the island so that she could get to know the place.

Maria didn't understand, they had given birth to children on this and all the other islands since time eternal without a midwife. But Karen Louise had authority and claimed that Barbro would need more help than others, she knew that from experience, Barbro wasn't like the others. Elise Havstein appeared to agree, at least she nodded in a way that meant it was unnecessary for her to say any more.

When the priest's wife had sketched out a kind of plan for the delivery, they shook hands again, the ladies were helped back on board the boat and the oarsmen rowed off.

Maria was left wondering why she hadn't offered them any coffee or food, no-one came here without being served refreshments.

She walked along the beach musing how she was going to tell the others the news, her daughter and her father-in-law. She decided to make a start with Ingrid, she was a big girl now. Her husband would have to be informed as soon as he returned from Lofoten. But she delayed going up to the house.

She removed her headscarf and walked along the beach towards the new quay, continued south to the sound of the babbling streams which had begun to carry the winter from the island out to sea. She sat down on a boulder, bared her feet and thrust them into the sea, waited until they were white and numb, pulled them out and dried them and her tears with the headscarf, put on her stockings and socks and went home and into the kitchen, where Ingrid was playing with her grandfather's hands, he was sitting in the rocking chair staring at Barbro as though waiting for the final proof that she was alive. Barbro didn't say anything. It was as if she hadn't come home and never would.

Maria went over and placed a hand on her shoulder and noticed that she smelled of roses, lilac and . . . nettles, noted that her hair had been cut and combed in the style women wore it in villages or on larger islands. She wondered if she should slap her, but her hand remained at her side. Barbro took it and held it tight and gazed into a well of despair, then let go, went into the pantry and came out again with the bread bin and said what she had missed most over there at the bloody rectory was decent food.

21

Since the frost had relinquished its grip and the wind was coming from the south-west, bringing heavy rain, mother and daughter moved back to the North Chamber. There, they could talk without having to keep looking over at the hole in the floor, beneath which Martin lay, he could hear everything they said.

Ingrid was told what she already knew, Barbro had spilled the beans on the first day, so they could have a mutual secret from Martin. But now her mother told her that when Ingrid was born her father had been afraid she would be like Barbro, it was in the family line, and every second or third generation they got a Barbro. But she, Maria, had seen that Ingrid was the way she was the moment she was born, it was her father who hadn't been sure about her, he was afraid.

"Hvafor?"

Maria took a deep breath and told Ingrid that it was her she could trust.

These were solemn words, and they were followed by no explanation, just some evasive phrases that had been locked inside her for so long that they were meant to stay there.

Ingrid was unable to bring herself to say anything.

They were at the end of the road.

But as the evening wore on she began to feel it was her mother she couldn't trust, as Maria had said something that frightened her, and had done nothing to dispel her fears, although she was allowed to knit now, no longer with an eiderdown over her shoulders, it was spring. Maria taught her how to knit the heel of a sock, by decreasing stitches, so that she would have a homecoming gift for her father when he came back from Lofoten.

Ingrid was seven years old.

But this incomplete conversation was not forgotten. And she still couldn't frame the question to ask her mother that would dispel her fears. A hard lump had formed inside Ingrid, she had a red dot hovering in front of her eyes which made her arms tremble, and then a bubble burst in the barn, when she was alone with Barbro, Barbro who had returned from the dead in someone else's clothes and with a child in her belly who didn't belong to anyone, either.

Barbro said that if Ingrid didn't stop crying she would become like her, it's like it's rainen' inside, an' oilskins won't help, it just makes tha more and more afraid, but tha can do somethin' about it.

Ingrid looked at her.

Barbro was shovelling muck through the hole in the wall and said that Ingrid would have to pull herself together, all those thoughts in her head were just a sign that she was growing up.

In the autumn she would be starting school on Havstein, with children from the other islands. From then on everything would be different, there is nothing to be afraid of, having nothing is something to be afraid of, but for that there are too many islands. The red dot went up in white smoke. Ingrid wrapped her arms around her aunt and never let her go.

22

Hans Barrøy had been worn out when he came home the previous year. Now he was stronger. The frost had devastated Lofoten too, but had not had much impact on line fishing. Now he had a quay on Barrøy. On his return, Uncle Erling's boat could not only come alongside, but also stay moored there for over twenty-four hours, using hawsers and spring lines. Ingrid was allowed to go on board even though she was a female, and was shown round the wheelhouse, cabins and galley, it was a floating house, which sailed under the name of *Barrøyværing* – Barrøy Islander.

The crew came ashore and was served food. Uncle Erling sat with his brother and father in the parlour drinking aquavit and coffee on a white tablecloth and eating *lefse*, and laughing louder than anyone had laughed here for four months, when Maria, through the open kitchen door, heard her husband enquire about the latest news and her father-in-law answer that they'd had a terrible frost but he had got through it, even though they had almost lost the mother ewes when the womenfolk herded them down to the beach to graze on seaweed.

Maria stood with the coffee pot in her hand.

She put it down, went to the hook by the door, where her father-in-law's red woolly hat was hanging, grabbed it and threw it in the stove.

She went into the parlour, poured the coffee, and told them what she had done, nobody will be wearing a red woolly hat anymore, it was old and grubby, and from now on Father-in-law was going to have a bath at least once a week, in the tub, in the barn, he was a pig. And one more thing: six of Barbro's new nets, complete with floats and sinkers and anchor ropes, were still strung across the sound like a dirty brown wall, south of the Swedes' boathouse, so Erling would have to watch out when he sailed south, and take the long route around Moltholmen.

They gaped at her.

Yes, and there was something else: in a month or so she would be going to Mo i Rana and staying there over the summer.

Mo i Rana?

Martin uttered a few expletives which were unfit for Ingrid's ears, once again she was sitting in her father's lap. Hans exchanged glances with his brother. Erling nodded. Hans put down his daughter and went into the kitchen.

From the parlour, it sounded as though they were having a normal conversation. The front door banged. Ingrid got up and from the parlour window saw her parents walking side by side across the spring-brown meadows. They were talking. Her father had his arm around her mother, her head lay on his shoulder, they were strolling hand in hand, then let go, now her mother walked with her arms crossed, her father with his hands in his pockets, they stopped and talked and looked around and went on and vanished. Ingrid hadn't noticed anything unusual, or alarming, neither had she seen anything she didn't understand, but she had seen something she would never forget.

From then on Martin had a regular bath in the barn. As regards the nets, he said, well, the frost had been so diabolical that there had been no question of taking them in, and after that he had forgotten all about them. He rowed out, cut through the furthermost anchor rope because he couldn't free the grapnel, and got the horse to drag the whole caboodle ashore. There it lay in a stinking heap throughout the summer, until it stopped stinking the following winter, after which it began to turn into earth, a circle of earth, between the smooth, bare rocks, where roseroot, sorrel and foxgloves would later grow. It looked strange, as if this mound of earth needed some reason to be there, or some explanation. Eventually, it was given a name at least, it was called Frosteye, Ingrid thought the name up.

Events turned out as Maria had predicted on the day of the homecoming, except the bit about Mo i Rana, which was never mentioned again. Those were words which never should have been spoken. For that very same reason they are not so quickly forgotten either, just like the things Maria told Ingrid about the family defect and her father, and what Barbro said about it raining inside and school and the other children who were like her, and growing up not being anything to be afraid of.

When Barbro gave birth, later that summer, with such suffering that Hans and Martin had to leave the house for more than a day and a night, it was Maria who delivered the baby. Elise Havstein arrived eight days late and was served coffee and cinnamon biscuits in the kitchen while the oarsmen were given crispbread with butter and syrup on the grass. It was fine weather that day. The men were also treated to some milk. And Elise the midwife stayed a long time. She saw to the baby boy, who was as round and white as a dumpling and cried whenever he couldn't suckle on Barbro, who had stopped working and had taken up residence in Martin's rocking chair. Barbro sang and breastfed. Elise Havstein had a daughter of Ingrid's age, whose name was Nelly and was also starting school that autumn, they were bound to become friends, there was no doubt about that. Elise Havstein stayed so long that the mountains on the mainland had turned blue before the flashing oar blades disappeared on the margin of their vision to the north. The boy was christened Lars, after the Swede Lars Klemet, who had been here with his workmates because of a war, and constructed a quay, before leaving again.

23

They are cutting peat. It has to be done between the peak periods on the farm, in June, so that the drying season is long. They use old scythe blades on which Hans has made a wooden handle. Only Hans uses a spade, he has whetted the blade, it is as sharp as a scythe. That is why he is the only person standing upright while he works. The others are on their knees in the bog. Barbro too. Her child is asleep on a sheepskin in the grass beside her.

The turfs of peat look like thick, black, wet books, they have to lie for a week in the heather until they form a crust and Hans and Martin can lay them in a circle and then build a round tower as high as a man with any number of little cracks like embrasures, then they toss the rest of the turfs into the cylinder, higgledy piggledy, and finish off at the top by working inwards to the centre, giving it a dome-shaped roof. It doesn't look like any other roof, on a house or a church, but not a single drop of rain can penetrate it, and the wind rushes in, through the crevices in the cylinder, like a thousand dry streams, then carries all the moisture out on the other side.

A correctly constructed peat stack is not only beautiful, like a man-made eye-catching attraction in the countryside, it is a work of art. A slapdash, hastily built stack, on the other hand, is a tragedy, which reveals its true nature at the worst possible moment, in January, when they wade through the snow with hand-woven baskets on their backs and discover the peat to be encrusted with ice, frozen rock solid. You have to attack it with a sledgehammer and an axe. With dynamite. And pick up the pieces for miles around and thaw them by the stove, only to find that what you have in your hands is not fuel but thick black mud, which is no use for anything. On top of that, you have to row a long way to the Trading Post and buy what is free of charge in your own bog, you can't get any more stupid than that.

Ingrid is the only person who doesn't cut, again she is too young, she turns half-dry turfs and stands them on their edges like dominoes in a fishbone pattern so the wind can slip between them and dry them out, the warm land wind that has blown over the island for many days now, but then it suddenly drops.

They all notice.

They stop working, gaze upwards and look at each other and listen.

There are no longer any bird screams either. There is no rustling in the grass and no insects are buzzing. The sea is smooth, the gurgling of water between the rocks on the beach has gone quiet, there isn't a sound between all the horizons, they are indoors.

A silence like this is very rare.

What is special about it is that it occurs on an island. It has more impact than the silence that can descend upon a forest without warning. A forest is often quiet. On an island there is so little silence that people stop what they are doing and look around and ask themselves what is going on. It makes them wonder. It is mystical, it borders on the thrilling, it is a faceless stranger in a black cloak wandering across the island with inaudible footsteps. The duration depends on the time of year, silence can last longer in the winter, with ice on the ground, while in summer there is always a slight pause between one wind and the next, between high and low tide or the miracle that takes place in humans as they change from breathing in to breathing out.

Then a gull screams again, a new puff of wind springs up from nowhere, and the well-fed child on the sheepskin wakes and bawls. They can pick up their tools and carry on working as if nothing has happened. For that is exactly what has happened: nothing. We talk about the calm before the storm, we say silence can be a warning, a call to action, or that it might mean we have to search in the Bible for a considerable time to understand its import. But silence on an island is nothing. No-one talks about it, no-one remembers it or gives it a name, however deep an impression it makes. It is the tiny glimpse of death they have while they are still alive.

24

This spring Hans Barrøy came back from Lofoten with new tools. They were stored in the boathouse where the Swedes had stayed. Two of the bunk beds have been removed and converted into one workbench with vices, which he had also brought with him. Martin came and examined the new planes, braces, drill bits, clamps and three different saw blades as well as a spirit level that could also be used vertically.

"All that thar must a cost tha a packet, eh?"

Hans didn't answer.

He had also brought back quite a few slim, pleasingly shaped pine mouldings, as golden as syrup, they had been unloaded with his nets and equipment. Now he held a pair of narrow brass hinges in front of his father's face and asked him if he missed his stupid woolly hat.

Martin put his hand to his bare scalp and was about to leave in anger. But all this happened after he had once again forgotten to take in the nets from the sea, so instead he went to get the boat, hauled the nets ashore and spent the rest of the day cleaning and hanging them up to dry on the rack behind the boat shed, it was like laundry the whole world was meant to see and admire.

Three days later they were woken by a terrible racket in the kitchen. Ingrid went down and saw that the window in the west-facing wall had been torn out and a new one was on its way in. Her father was putting in blocks and wedges, levelling up and hammering in nails, then filling in and cladding, inside and outside, and there was also a sill. It was a hinged window. A window with two sections, which could be opened.

Outside, he screwed in two hasps and made a wedge for each so that the windows wouldn't bang in the wind when they were left open. This should have been done in Martin's day, like so much else, because they didn't have a bakehouse on Barrøy, they baked in the kitchen and had to keep the door open to let out the steam, and it didn't want to go. Now they could open the window instead. It was left open for most of the summer, also when it was drizzling, because like everything else that was new, it had to be in use all the time. Then they closed it. But it could still be opened, such as when, a few months later, Maria had to shout to her people working in the potato field that dinner was ready.

"Go an' wash tha mitts."

The other change was bigger. It concerned the new quay, which still lacked a decent building, a house. In August, materials were delivered in the Trading Post's cargo boat and piled under an old sail away from the shore. Maria went and counted them up and worked out what they cost, but said nothing, in fact she never did say anything.

And Hans pretended he didn't hear.

He and his father hammered and sawed for a month, made the roof trusses on the ground and hoisted them aloft one by one using a block and tackle, then started to board the house at the beginning of September. They discussed which wall to start with and agreed to tackle the long, south-west-facing wall first, most of the weather came from this direction, so they would have some shelter while they clad the rest of the house. Martin noticed that he had a say in reaching this decision.

The morning they were about to start on the first gable wall the wind picked up. Hans took a look at the weather and decided there was nothing any human could do.

They walked home and watched from the new kitchen window as the storm tore their construction to pieces, like matchsticks, and hurled it north into the fjord. The gales died down in the course of the night. The next morning they put to sea in the *færing* and rowed around collecting whatever they could find. They landed on islets and skerries and also spoke to Thomas on Stangholmen, who had seen what had happened through his binoculars and had been out gathering some of the materials that drifted his way. They salvaged almost everything.

The following day they set about laying another bottom beam in the same place. But this one they bolted down more securely. By the beginning of October a new framework was in place. A week later the south-west-facing wall was weather-boarded for the second time. They used more stays and diagonal braces than it needed. As they did with the other walls. At the end of the month the first snow arrived. By then they had clad four walls and were in the process of finishing the wooden roof structure.

However, one afternoon something strange happened to the sky, and when the sky not only goes dark but also strange and is low and hard to read, this is a sign in itself, a sign of the worst. They spent the next hour tying down the construction with whatever wires and rope they could find. Immediately after the onset of darkness the first crash broke over the island.

By which time they were indoors.

And this time they wouldn't have to witness the destruction. It happened in the depths of night. But they could hear the noise. This storm was also more severe and nigh on two days and nights passed before they could row out to hunt for their materials. This time they found much less. Hans estimated that after three days of searching they had salvaged roughly sixty per cent of the house and a lot of the timber was so battered that it could be used only as firewood.

Next day they bolted down a new bottom beam, but on this occasion the building was turned ninety degrees and would have the gables in the north and south and the long wall facing the quay to the west. They thought it would look ridiculous. But they weren't making the rules anymore. By the time the frost came at the beginning of December the basic framework was complete for the third time with the roof trusses two foot or so lower than originally planned. But by now they had run out of materials. They used the last they had on the braces, left the exposed lathed framework as one big white Christmas present and went home, the winter would determine the outcome, if the bloody thing was still standing in spring they could finish the cladding then.

But the following day was just as calm.

They sat in the kitchen looking out at the pale morning darkness, at the new creation over on the Hammer, it no longer looked like a Christmas present but a block of ice, on all sides the sea lay black and mucilaginous like glue beneath a starless sky.

Hans got up and went into the pantry, where the calendar hung, and read that today was St Barbro's day, December 4. He had to smile, came back and opened the window and looked out, it was like another silence. Complete and unchanging, a hum of peace, which makes you believe that it might last, and after exchanging a few words with his father they put on their outdoor clothes and walked down to the boat shed, launched the *færing*, took the larger rowing boat in tow and rowed to the Trading Post. There they loaded the boat with all the materials they could get, bought twelve kilos of nails, a tin of coffee and twenty kilos of flour, rowed back and that same afternoon set about cladding the south-west-facing wall. They finished just after midnight.

They slept a few hours and were there to meet the cargo boat the next morning, it was carrying more materials. They clad the next wall during the day and evening and ate the food Maria and Barbro brought to the site. They also worked through the next night. A day and a night later all the walls were finished. The old kitchen window was put in the north-facing gable wall, two big doors opened up onto the quay and the second long wall had a narrow door which faced the old Lofoten boat shed. The two buildings seemed to be staring at each other. Now it was time to start on the roof structure.

It took them two full days.

Maria and Barbro carried more food to the building site and also passed up materials from the ground. Hans and Martin nailed down two broad planks for the roof ridge. Then two more. Thereafter they laid the battens, and the question arose as to what roof covering they should have. It should be slate, Hans decided, he had seen it on many houses in Lofoten, also on the mainland, he would buy some there this winter and have it transported home in Erling's boat.

Martin didn't like the idea of slate, it blew off, like the pages of a book without a spine, and was lost in the sea. But his son wouldn't listen. He was busy drilling holes in the rock for two steel cables which would stretch up to the eaves, complete with turnbuckles, making the quay house resemble the rigging on a schooner. It was the only building on the island that had stays. They didn't know yet if it would be progress or a fiasco, only winter would tell.

But the weather stayed calm from Christmas to the New Year, including when Uncle Erling moored and everyone stood watching Hans loading his fishing tackle and equipment. This time, though, Martin helped with the line tubs. And Barbro had her child in her arms, little Lars, kicking his legs and laughing. Ingrid noticed that it was no longer heartbreaking to say goodbye to her father. At most it was sad. They waved, went home, and their loneliness began.

25

Ingrid has started school. Her mother rows her there on the first day. Over to Havstein. They laugh a lot on the way. Maria has something to tell her, from her own schooldays, she seems to miss them. Ingrid asks her if she was once a child too. Maria laughs and says yes and suddenly seems to be a mixture of a secret and a question. Then she declares that she didn't have such a good father as Ingrid has. Ingrid asks if her mother's father was a bad man. Maria says no. Ingrid cannot think of anything else to ask, and Maria has no more to tell.

They row into a flock of puffins, and she asks Ingrid to count the colours on their bills. Ingrid says that is boring, she has done it before. She too does some rowing. Because it is a long way. Afterwards she sits on the forward thwart and can feel her mother's back against her own as Havstein rises from the sea, a strip of land with lots of houses. One of them is white. It is the farmhouse on Havstein estate, where school is to be held this term, with teachers and fifteen pupils, eight of them new. They each come from a different island, some are bigger than others, but they are all small.

They have to sleep in the loft of the farmhouse for two

weeks, then they are home for the following two weeks while Olai Christoffer Christoffersen teaches on another island. When he has taught the new children to put up their hands and ask for permission to say something before they say something, he asks his first question, can they swim?

The new children look at each other in puzzlement, the more experienced glance down at their writing boards. Ingrid puts up her hand and says her mother can swim.

"You're going to learn too, today," the teacher says in a strange dialect, because they are islanders and for islanders swimming is as important as being able to sail and row and pray. He orders the new pupils into the yard where they are to line up in two rows.

They do as he says and are marched to a bay on the far side of the island where they find a sandy beach as white as the one Ingrid has at home on Barrøy. But the beach here forms almost a complete circle and is very shallow everywhere, at low tide it is dry, so the sun can warm the sand, which then heats the water when the tide comes in. Along the eastern bank there is a level shelf of rock, as though a road has been hewn from the mountainside. The teacher stands there with a long bamboo cane – even longer than the boathook Ingrid's father uses to haul straggling fish on board – and orders them to go into the water in their underwear.

It is cold, though still warm for the sea. In turn they hold the end of the cane as the teacher steps up onto the rock and gives instructions they can't understand. He pulls them to and fro through the water like wriggling white fish. They splash their feet and are scolded until they do it correctly. Then they stand still with the water up to their necks making swimming strokes until finally they have to duck their heads under the water, again and again, if anyone doesn't do it they get a whack with the cane; in this way they learn to hold their breath, it is an art in itself.

Eventually they have to lunge forward and perform the movements they have learned with their arms and legs, because now that they can hold their breath, it doesn't matter whether they hold their heads above or below the water. The teacher looks at his watch and the sun and the tide marker and they are not allowed to get out of the water until they all have blue lips and their teeth are chattering.

"That was a good start," he says.

They march back to the farm in wet underwear, enter from the rear so that no-one sees them and go up to the loft where they will be sleeping, boys in the north, girls in the south, and where they find a number of washing lines stretched across the rooms for them to hang their wet clothes, after which they can put on the second set of clothing they have been advised to bring from home.

After three days they can all swim, and a competition is held. In pouring rain they have to swim across the bay and back again, then grab the bamboo stick which is now floating like a yellow snake between two pieces of rope beneath the rock shelf where the teacher stands and where he at length can confirm that Nelly Elise is the winner. She is the daughter of the mid-wife. As it is absurd that a girl should win, the teacher rules that she could already swim before she arrived at the school. Nelly has a stammer, so she does not complain. Nor does she say anything in the classroom, however much the teacher admonishes her, and he does so with fervour, until he finally gives up. Nelly is strong.

Ingrid isn't. She enjoys being with the others and isn't frightened at all, only excited, and laughs all the time. But she isn't allowed to. You are not allowed to laugh in the classroom, for three reasons, the teacher counts on his long, thin fingers: it is disruptive, it is infectious and it looks stupid.

You are not allowed to laugh when you are eating, either.

Ingrid doesn't understand what he means. Not being allowed to laugh when you need to is like being deprived of a leg.

But life is hell, she does learn that at least, so she stops laughing and starts crying instead. Every night. She shares a bed with Nelly, who still won't speak, and in her heart yearns to be home on Barrøy. The red dot is back. She gets out of bed and runs half-naked into the rain and around the house, down to the harbour and up again and towards the beach where they learned to swim. Without meeting a single person. Then back again, because Havstein is an island too, no matter how well you can swim or row. She goes up to the loft and takes off her wet clothes and hangs them on the line and puts on dry ones and gets back into bed and cries until Nelly opens her mouth and tells her to shut up. She also says:

"Tha h-h-has nice h-h-hair."

She asks if she can brush and plait Ingrid's hair. She can. Tonight and every other night. Ingrid can't say no. And when Maria comes to collect Ingrid the following week her mother says the same:

"Hvur lovely tha hair is." As though discovering her daughter for the first time. On the way home she also says:

"Hvur serious tha is."

Ingrid doesn't tell her much about her first two weeks in hell, about how she cried and threw up and felt a burning in her insides and fainted twice. Instead she tells Maria that she has learned to swim, that they have doors with keyholes and rooms you are not allowed to enter, she has learned the alphabet and numbers and seen herself in a big mirror they have hanging in the farmhouse, once when the door wasn't locked.

Maria studies her, as though searching for something.

Nelly has taught Ingrid not to say anything because what is odd about contagion is that it can encompass both good and bad. And now she has a fortnight off. At this time her father and grandfather are constructing the first building for the new quay. She is allowed to be with them every day and passes them nails and the spirit level that her father brought from Lofoten, the instrument that ensures that whatever has to be plumb is plumb and whatever has to be level is level.

26

Martin says that there is a reason for Hestskjæret being known as Horse Reef, and for Oksholmen, Bull Island, being surrounded by dangerous waters. These animal names are warnings, signs to disguise the reefs' real names and true nature, they are tokens of the Devil, of Satan. They also have a Bukkeskjær, Goat Reef, and a Værholme, Ram Island. For the same reason. Hooved animals. Four-legged beasts. Having a horse on board a boat, for example, goes against every instinct, and happens only in extremis, when they are being transported. Just think of the hell it is getting a breeding bull here or when the cows have to leave, it is never a normal job, there is quite simply something that is not right about the whole operation, you can feel it in your body.

His son is sick of this talk, he thinks it is old man's blather and an irrational belief, the opposite of true faith, which is founded in God, who rules over fate and the weather and fish, as anyone can confirm. Superstition, however, is based on idiocy.

But Hans has become more pensive since his daughter started school, the old disquiet is back, caused by the reticence she has acquired, and that strange gravity that has taken residence in her eyes. And while they are sitting on the pile of boards in a break from work, his gaze falls on the horse grazing in Rose Acre, and he asks his father, as though the time is finally ripe, do they actually need this creature, a horse?

It is inside for eight of the twelve months and tucks away enough fodder for one and a half cows, it pulls the mower and the plough and a cartload of hay, but they usually carry the turfs of peat themselves, so is the horse actually just something they have got used to, like a bad habit, a ball and chain?

It is old too, ancient.

Martin can see that his son has moved towards his position, it is a kind of admission, since Martin was critical of this investment, so he says the horse was a wise acquisition when it arrived, even though it came by boat, how else would they have got it here . . . ? And leaves the rest of the reasoning hanging in the air for Hans to draw his own conclusions.

Hans goes into the Lofoten boat shed and fetches the gun, they lead the horse down to the marsh to the west – you don't let the women in a house see that you are killing a horse – and shoot it and bury it where it falls, like a breeding ram. It takes them the rest of the day and a good part of the next. But they don't let up, they say: bloody animal, and wipe the sweat from their brows and go back to the building site and carry on working, they have already started cladding the south wall and look forward to finishing this so that they are sheltered while completing the rest of the house.

But Hans Barrøy still feels a disquiet when he looks at his

daughter or casts his eye over the island and notes that every-thing is not as it was before. At all waking hours of the day he knows where the animals are, every single one, for there are eagles and steep slopes here, but now he keeps catching himself straightening his back and searching for the absent horse before he realises it is dead, before he carries on working.

It happens again and again.

He is reflecting on the force of habit and wondering whether he regrets killing the horse when he sees the sky fill with turbu-lence, this is the first storm, which is going to demolish the new building at any moment.

All you can do is start again.

After the storm has flattened the second building too, Hans Barrøy begins to read the Bible. He takes it with him to Lofoten and leafs through it on shore days and public holidays. When, in April, they steer the boat southwards again with the flag flying aloft, to signal to those waiting that everyone is returning safe and sound once more, he regards it as a lucky omen that the framework of the new building on the Hammer is still intact, just as he left it in the winter darkness four months previously, only a little greyer. In the hold there is a stack of slate tiles with which he will soon cover the roof.

He doesn't draw any grand conclusions from the bold new building having survived, but is filled with enormous relief, and on top of everything his daughter is standing on the quay holding a little boy's hand and pointing to the flag on the mast and whispering something in his ear. Hans can see the old smile on her face, which almost brings him to his knees, even though she isn't a son. This year he has presents with him from Lofoten as well, he didn't have any last year, then he had tools and window materials, this winter he has had other things on his mind.

There is also a present for Martin, a razor with an ivory handle. The others get dress material and sugar and Ingrid a music box and a book called *The Good Samaritan and the Donkey*. There is nothing for Lars.

Ingrid also gets a mirror. This is the third time she has seen herself in a mirror. The first was on Havstein last year. In addition, she has been allowed to play with one her mother has in her chest and usually doesn't take out, this was when she came home from school one day with red dots in front of her eyes and wouldn't eat.

Now she can look at herself as much as she wants.

She also lets Lars look in the mirror, without him realising what is going on. And the cat and her grandfather, and her father shows her, when she is sitting in front of it writing, how her right hand becomes her left and the letters become illegible, she is the other way round, as though it were possible to be someone else while still being yourself.

She goes upstairs and puts it away in the wooden chest she has in her room.

All women have a wooden chest, they have had these for longer than they have had chairs. On the lid of Ingrid's a name has been engraved, PETRINE, and a year. Petrine was Hans's maternal grandmother. But it is Maria who sees to it that the contents are as they should be. If they aren't, she may remove something.

You don't need that, she says, about, say, a headscarf or a cup or a tablecloth, and replaces it with something from her own chest. This too Ingrid will inherit one day. So the question is whether it is necessary to move anything from one chest to the other. But it is. This is all about time and age, about two family lines merging into one. Ingrid's chest is more or less as it should be, she and Maria are almost in agreement about that.

When Hans and Maria walk around the island and he sees everything again, he doesn't mention that he has thought a lot about the horse over the winter, but intimates he may have become a little more devout. He also says it is good to be home again, they even have a special word for this: home-loving. This isn't necessarily a positive quality for a man, so Maria says he is assuredly neither more devout nor home-loving, only older, he has some grey hair on his temples.

He feels a surprising relief, which has nothing to do with this matter, and notices that a few grey hairs have appeared on Maria's head, too. But when they walk up the last slope on their way back to the houses, once again he catches himself feeling that there is something missing, an animal, a horse.

He stops and asks how many lambs they had in spring and hears her counting and pointing them out. He walks in amongst them and counts himself and hears the names they have given them and knows that from now on nothing will be as it was. A year has passed, it won't come back, and if he asks Maria how Ingrid is doing she will say what she always does, it is as if he still doesn't trust what he can see with his own eyes.

27

Lars was no more than seven months old when he pulled himself up by grabbing Barbro's nets and after swaying for a few moments fell backwards and hit his head on the floor. This happened several times. A week later he could stand upright holding on to a cod net and look around the kitchen. Lars loved standing.

Ingrid packed snow round the lower half of his body so that he could stand outside and wave his arms. He had blond, almost butter-yellow hair, brown eyes and chubby red cheeks. He was only eight months when he was able to stand up on the kitchen floor without any help and walk and fall and get up again and stand and walk and fetch something to eat from the pantry, because although he didn't talk much he understood what they said and knew the difference between cup and spoon and the little tin box.

When the snow was gone he could walk from the house to the barn and the furthest peat stack. In March the ground was covered with a sheet of ice. It rained, the frost returned, and a new coating of ice lay over the island, so they had to wear cleats on their boots. Ingrid pulled the toddler on the sledge across the flattest fields, she also threaded some fish hooks through some old *lugg* boots and made cleats for him too, it was like teaching him to walk again.

At the beginning of April he went missing, first once, then again, both times they found him on Kvitsanda beach, where he sat digging the sand with a stick. At lambing time they had to attach him to a rope in the yard. But when Ingrid was home from school she would look after him from when he got up till when he went to bed. Otherwise he was with his grandfather in the boat shed playing with glass floats and fishing lines or sitting in a line tub eating dry bread. The day before Hans returned from Lofoten, Martin thrust the boy's hand into a bucket of tar and got him to make two prints on the boat-shed wall, two small right hands that resembled the heads of hares and would remain there forever.

The tar remained on his hand, too, so before they rowed over to mass on Whit Sunday, Barbro scrubbed it so hard it turned bright red and had to be hidden under a mitten. Lars walked on his own from the boat up to the church. Afterwards they arranged with Pastor Johannes Malmberget for the boy to be christened on the first Sunday in August, although they had to admit he didn't have a father.

"We all have a father," Johannes Malmberget said. "We are the children of nature."

These words are actually lies that are intended merely to console, because everyone comes from two places, and Lars was, firstly, the son of a foreigner and secondly of Barbro, and therefore had a double cloud of suspicion hanging over him. But also some expectations and hope. However, as he grew in the course of the year, both the suspicion and the hope faded, only to reappear whenever he broke something or performed some great feat, and basically he did neither.

He ran down from the churchyard to the beach and stood watching his grandfather, who had gone ahead of him and sat on a thwart with his back turned, his face hidden in his hands. The old man heard the boy splashing in the water, but didn't stir.

The others followed and found him sitting in the same rigid position. As Lars had waded out into the sea and was up to his waist in water, they realised something was wrong.

Maria asked what the matter was.

Martin muttered between his fingers that that was the last time he was going to church. They asked him why. He didn't answer, but when they enquired whether it was because of Kaja's grave, he nodded and replied that he didn't want to read the writing on her headstone again, they should never have put that verse of poetry there, the priest was right, they had to remove it.

Maria called him a silly old ass and told him to budge up. The rest of the family climbed on board and Lars was wrapped in a blanket. On the way home, Ingrid asked what all the fuss was about in connection with her grandmother's gravestone, but didn't receive an answer. She repeated the question. Maria asked her why she kept nagging her. Ingrid wouldn't give in. Maria said she didn't know, she had never known her mother-in-law, Ingrid would have to ask her father. Ingrid asked her father. He smiled and said it was a beautiful verse, Ingrid's grandmother knew what she was doing. Ingrid nodded and looked in turn from her mother to her grandfather, who was sitting at the front of the boat with his back to them, staring down at his hands.

When they landed by the boat shed he said what the hell was the point of that hulking great quay with the new building when they had only two *færings* and two rowing boats.

Maria shook her head.

Hans said nothing. Barbro held Lars aloft and tickled him. Martin walked up to the houses, and Ingrid felt sorry for him. This was a completely new sensation. She had no idea where it came from. The following day it had gone. But it resurfaced at times when she was preoccupied with quite different thoughts. On these occasions she recognised it as the sensation she experienced on that trip home from the churchyard, the strokes of the oars, and the faces. But she never got accustomed to it, and never told anyone about it.

28

Ingrid is sitting in the big reception room in Havstein Manor with a board on her lap, her knees together, holding a slate pencil and looking out of the window at a low February sun that will soon be leaving the uneven pane. She has finished writing. She knows that every word has been spelled correctly. She can feel the heat from the stove, she knows that her mittens are hanging up with the others', her boots are standing with the others' and her outer clothes are hanging in the hall with the others'. She is one of the others. She is from one island, and the others are from a different island. They are together. She no longer laughs when she is not supposed to, she has her hair plaited. She fixes her eyes on Olai, the teacher, until he can feel her gaze and looks up.

But he doesn't say anything. They wait. For the others who are still writing. Then he asks in a whisper over three bowed heads if she has finished. Ingrid nods. He nods too and continues writing in the register while Ingrid returns her gaze to the window, where the sun glides from the pane and slips into a dark triangle on the sand-scrubbed floor, the sail of a boat drifting through the room and taking the day with it, soon Gabriel will be here with the lanterns, Gabriel is a silent kindly spirit and the oldest member of the family, it is Saturday and Ingrid is going home.

But for the first time she is not eager to leave.

She puts down the board, gets up without asking permission and walks over and places her slate on the teacher's desk and sees his surprised expression, turns anyway and fetches her clothes and boots and takes her little bag and leaves the room, still without asking permission or so much as a glance.

She puts on her coat in the hall and walks out into the cold, ten minutes before school finishes – she has seen the time on the big wall clock – and continues down to the harbour, where her grandfather is talking to two men of the same age and laughing at something or other. It is the first time she has not longed to go home. It is the first time she has not been afraid. She is nine. And she notices her grandfather is different with strangers from how he is at home. She is too, she thinks.

She stands in front of him with a smile. He returns her smile. He pats her cheek. Then he drops his large hand and keeps on talking to the two men as though nothing has happened, so Ingrid goes down to the *færing* and sits waiting on the middle thwart. Martin doesn't come, he is talking.

Ingrid gets up and steps forward to untie the mooring rope, then sits at the oars, starts rowing and is well out in the harbour before her grandfather spots her and runs up and down the wharf shouting. He waves his arms and shouts that she should come back for him. But she doesn't. Ingrid is rowing. There is no wind, the sea is dead calm, the islets are white with black edges, the water is green. She rows with long, powerful strokes, like her mother, and is halfway home before an unfamiliar boat with two oarsmen catches up with her, whereupon her grandfather jumps on board the *færing*, unsure whether to give her a mouthful or laugh, she can see that in his face, this old man whom she knows better than anyone else. He tells her that now she will have to row all the bloody way home, as for him, he is going to sit on the stern thwart and smoke.

29

When Barbro grew up on Barrøy girls didn't have chairs. They stood at the table and ate. Of the women in the house it was only her mother, Kaja, who sat, and she didn't start doing that until she'd had her first son. When Kaja died Barbro wanted her chair. But Hans wanted to give it to Maria, whom he had just married. Shortly afterwards, his elder brother, Erling, got married as well and moved to another, wealthier island. As a result both Barbro and Maria got a chair, at roughly the same time. And when Ingrid was only three her father made a chair for her too, with arms they could lay a board over, so that she could sit on it with her feet on the seat, until she was big enough to sit without it.

An era was over.

None of this was discussed. There is no knowing whether this was Barbro's demand or an idea Hans had brought back with him from Lofoten, which led to the women in the house being able to sit as well. It was just done, the way people suddenly find a new way through the wilderness and like it and go that way again and after a while establish a path, which is just another word for a habit.

But Barbro remembers what it was like not to have a chair, so, once she had it, she took it with her everywhere she went, to the old boat shed and the Swedes' boathouse, and also into the fields, she sat on it and watched the animals and the sky, and the oystercatchers on the shore. A piece of furniture outdoors. That makes the sky a ceiling and the horizon walls in a house called the world. No-one had done this before. The others could never get used to it, either.

So another chair had to be made, for Lars. Hans made it on his new workbench in the boathouse. Barbro kept a watchful eye on him. She took him coffee and food. He tried to chase her away.

But she just stood outside and waited, and he couldn't allow her to stand in the rain, so he told her to come back in and sweep up the wood shavings and put away his tools when he no longer needed them.

It turned out to be the finest chair on the island. Like Ingrid's, with arms you could place a board on, but also with some carvings at the top of the backrest, which looked like the petals of a flower no-one had ever seen. There was also an oval hole in the seat, which Lars could shit through, into a potty, it was both a chair and a toilet, until he was big enough to go to the latrine the others used, which was next to the barn.

30

Occasionally they receive visitors from the other islands. Then their guests are served food and coffee and talk non-stop and all at the same time, for words build up in the islanders and at some point have to come out. When they are empty they go home again and begin to collect new things to say. But no strangers ever come on casual visits.

So what is this?

It starts as a grey shadow distinguishable against the shimmering waves in the east and gradually taking the form of a boat. Hans sees it first, it has no sail, there is only one man on board, and it is still so far away that they have plenty of time to find out everything about him before he arrives. Firstly, he is in unknown waters, no doubt about that, and he is no dab hand at rowing, so he must be from the mainland?

But there is something purposeful about his rowing, as if it is here, Barrøy, and nowhere else, that he is heading for, so they have to ask themselves whether he has heard something about them which has made him come, or whether he knows them or might be a distant relative.

But they have no acquaintances or family on the mainland.

So does he want to sell them something? This has never happened before, but it can't be ruled out. Or could it be a message he has to deliver?

However, usually Thomas on Stangholmen does this, or one of the oarsmen from the Trading Post. But if this were the case, what might this message be? News of someone's death?

Hans goes through the names of those closest to him who might have died, and comes to the conclusion that they wouldn't send a stranger, but of course there are other types of message . . .

Such as?

Then they recognise the boat, it is the *færing* belonging to Adolf from Malvika, at the foot of the mountain on the mainland, and Adolf never lends his boats to anyone, especially not to people who can't row and don't know where they are. In other words, a wave of uncertainty precedes this new arrival until, on top of it all, they discover that he looks scary standing there in the rocking boat with his long black hair and beard and eyes that look in different directions.

Their first impulse is to chase him away. But they are polite and curious and stand passively watching him step ashore and listen to him speaking loudly and rapidly in a dialect they are unfamiliar with. He tells them he has escaped from somewhere, from jail, he says, and begs them to take pity on him.

"I can see you're simple folk, who are not accustomed to people like me, I could do as I please here, but I have no wish to do so, I'd prefer to partake of your hospitality . . ."

Hans is comforted to hear that the stranger seems cultured. And his voice is reassuring, maybe because it would have been worse with mere silence, in addition to his wild appearance. Hans nods to the rest of his family to set their minds at rest, but says to the stranger:

"Tha can't bide hier."

Then everything changes.

"A tol' tha A'm bidin' hier," he replies, mimicking their dialect with a snort, slings a kitbag over his shoulder and abandons the boat without mooring it, then walks up toward the houses, leaving the family there, gaping spectators to an invasion of their own kingdom.

Martin wades out and grabs the mooring rope. They pull the boat ashore and exchange glances, rotate it half a turn so the broad painted side is visible from the sea, Adolf's *færing* on dry land where it doesn't belong, that is meant as a signal, a cry for help, which they don't even believe in themselves.

They walk up in the footsteps of a convict, all their eyes on Hans, he can sense it, and when they see the stranger going into the house as though he lived there, he knows what he has to do, he has to kill this man.

There is a kind of gathering outside the door, in truth no more than collective hesitancy, Hans goes in first, then Maria and Ingrid and Barbro with Lars on her arm, even though he is four and squirming and wants to be put down.

Martin stays outside and stands by the casement window, where he sees the family standing in a line against the wall inside, like beggars in their own kitchen, while the intruder has commandeered Hans's chair and eyes them up one by one, considering what orders to give his servants next.

"Hvo's tha?" he says to Ingrid. They don't know whether he is making fun of them or not. Ingrid lets go of her mother's hand, steps forward and says her name. The stranger nods, but doesn't appear to have hit on anything interesting to ask her to do, instead he turns his attention to Barbro and repeats the question. Barbro doesn't answer.

"Haven't tha any grub?"

They understand the words, but remain motionless, as if they don't know where things are, the pantry door, the stove, the chimney pipe, the coffee grinder and the jars of salt, sugar . . . the tubs on the bench next to the sink that Hans had brought from Lofoten that spring, it is as if they haven't seen these before, and the intruder not only looks as though he lives here, he even seems to feel at home. He repeats the word "grub", they recoil, and only Ingrid has the presence of mind to ask what he would like.

He answers in a loud voice, as if they are deaf, says they must have some bread, butter, meat . . . I saw some cows out there, calves . . .

Maria opens the pantry door. The stranger shouts something to her. She stops and looks over her shoulder. And now Hans can't stand there any longer. He leaves his three women-folk and one nephew and goes out without heeding the words the new owner shouts at him, though they ring in his ears:

"Where the hell d'you think you're going?"

He goes down to the potato field, where they broke off their work when the boat came into view, and sits down with his back to the house.

Ingrid can see him from the window. Her grandfather follows Hans and sits down at his side. They talk. It has started to rain. Barbro settles down in the rocking chair with the large child on her lap, eyes the stranger, who eyes her back, aping her, Barbro rocks back and forth, pinches Lars to make him sit still, while the interloper looks as if he is about to explode as Maria places food on the table. Now Ingrid cannot bear to be there any longer either.

She looks down at her hands, blackened with soil, but can't bring herself to leave without asking for permission. And she doesn't ask her mother but the stranger, who has been given bread and cold fish and butter, she asks if she can go.

He says she can do what she likes.

She curtsies, goes out, down to the potato field, and stands in front of her father, who is on his knees between the furrows furiously tossing potatoes into a box, which she has never seen him do before. Hans Barrøy is not a man to kneel, the women lift the potatoes, he transports the boxes to the cellar. Now he seems to be praying. Ingrid stands there until he asks her what she is staring at.

He repeats the question.

Behind him she sees her grandad sitting with his hands on his knees. He is shaking his head. Her father struggles to his feet and raises his hand as if intending to hit her. She feels no fear. He lowers his hand and casts a sidelong glance at his father, who comes over and stands at his side.

They exchange a few words. Ingrid blinks.

They leave the Garden of Eden shoulder to shoulder, walk across to the quay, disappear into the Lofoten boat shed and re-emerge, Hans carrying the harpoon gun they use to shoot porpoises, his father a sledgehammer shaft, after which they return to the house and go inside.

Ingrid wants to stop them, but cannot utter a sound, runs after them and stands outside the kitchen window peering through the rain-wet pane, unable to see anything. She is walking towards the porch when the door opens again and out comes the stranger, backwards, suddenly he seems smaller.

After him comes first her father, with the gun to his shoulder and the kitbag in his hand, he flings it at the stranger. Then comes Barbro, still with Lars on her arm, and finally her grandfather, who takes an unsteady stride off the doorstep, falls forward and hits the stranger in the face with the hammer shaft causing him to fall, too, with a loud cry.

Ingrid sees her father rest the weapon against his shoulder and close one eye. Maria places a hand on his arm. Grandad gets to his feet again. The stranger has blood on his face, he is cursing, and then there is something about his clothes, which they hadn't noticed before, he is smartly dressed, in an expensive suit, a waistcoat with shiny buttons, trousers with a sharp crease, a gold chain dangling from one pocket, a rich man backing off southwards through the meadows with the whole pack of them after him.

When they get to the boat they stand around looking at one another.

He wipes a hand over his face and gives a shrug. They watch him slide out the boat while Hans keeps his gun trained on him. They watch him climb aboard, sit at the oars and begin to row with the same clumsy strokes that brought him here, heading first towards Malvika and the mountains, where he came from, then north-east towards the Trading Post. He disappears in a grey shower of rain, reappears and vanishes for good in even more rain.

They are drenched. They know nothing about him, what his name is, where he came from, nor where he is going. All they know is that he has been there. Ingrid looks at her father, who doesn't return her gaze, but walks arm in arm with Maria back to the house, the gun under his arm, with Martin wielding the hammer shaft, while Barbro finally puts Lars down so that he can run about as he usually does.

The following night Ingrid is woken by the sound of boats coming from all directions, it is no use turning over, it is no use looking away, closing your eyes, forgetting, breaking into a run, for her feet move as little as her eyelids.

She goes into her parents' room and wakes Maria, sees from her mother's face that she will tell her to go back. But she changes her mind and gets up, goes to Ingrid's room and lies

137

down beside her, Ingrid and Maria, she asks if the man will come back.

"No," her mother says.

That was what she said when Barbro left.

And next day, when Ingrid sees her father casting his eye around in the potato field, as if on the lookout for a boat, or a horse, and he says that he is sorry he didn't kill the bastard, it was stupid of him to let him escape in a boat that didn't belong to him, Adolf's boat, she can't understand why they didn't do it. Nothing has been taken from the island, nothing has been stolen or destroyed. Yet the stranger has robbed them of the most important thing they had, which they can never regain. Ingrid believes it has something to do with the different ways they reacted, those who left the kitchen because they couldn't bear to be there, and those who stayed. Ingrid is a sentimental child.

31

Hans Barrøy treads on a nail and injures a toe, it turns septic. He limps more and more with every day that passes and has to go to a hospital on the mainland and have it amputated. On his return, he walks with a stick, they have cut off not one toe but two, because he left it so late, and now he can't travel to Lofoten, Maria decides.

"Hva a we goen' t' live on?"

"Tha can't go t' sea with a stick," she says.

Uncle Erling completely agrees when he drops by in his boat at the start of the New Year. Hans will have to let one of the men see to the fishing tackle this winter, he says, take a half-catch share in payment and stay at home, fish close to the shore, with tha stick, ha ha.

Hans acquiesces and sends Erling off with half of his gear, he remains on the new quay with his family watching the *Barrøyværing* depart without him for the first time in fifteen years.

This happens on the morning of January 3.

Those who have to go to work in the barn, go to the barn. While Hans stands looking around him. It is a curious situation and there is nothing to look at. There is the horizon, here is the land. He can hear the sea. But that is it. Now he walks away to collect all the materials he can find and starts making benches in the new boathouse. He continues without a break until he is finished the following day. Two benches. Then he tells Barbro he wants to teach her how to bait lines.

"A know hvur t' do that already," Barbro says.

"But tha's got t' bi able t' mend 'em too," Hans says. "And coil 'em up neat."

Barbro can't do that. Barbro likes to put bits of herring onto the hooks and tries to wind the lines carefully into the tub, but the tangles get worse the more she struggles. But Ingrid can do it well, when she isn't at school. And Maria too, when she isn't in the cowshed or cooking.

It was a strange winter, a winter without emptiness, loneliness or gravity. The finest winter in Ingrid's life, nothing short of a summer. Even the weather was as it should be. Hans and Martin got up at the crack of dawn every morning, as in the busiest periods of the year, ran four tubs of line across the water between Barrøy and Havstein and fished on the seaward side of the island whenever the weather permitted. They also fished with nets.

More and more nets.

In the middle of January the first fish-drying rack saw the light of day. They hadn't had a rack on Barrøy before, apart from the one where they dried the nets. First there was one, then a second. By the end of March they had three, all on the hills in the west. There they dried the twelve tons of fish they caught in the course of these months, and that is not bad for two men and two and a half women in the baiting room, that amounts to almost three tons of dried fish. When the weather was bad they were forced to stay on land, and it was Maria who had the final word on what constituted bad weather. Things were going so well that they could stay home at the merest hint of a gale.

But again Hans regretted he had got rid of the horse, because they had to carry the pairs of tail-tied fish to the rack by hand.

He gave this a lot of thought. Having a horse still wasn't economically viable, with all the fodder it consumed. The family carried the fish in crates which Hans strapped to their backs, and Lars dragged fish after him in the snow, a pair in each hand. It was a terrible slog. But can't we move the racks to behind the quay house where they clean and tie the fish, for Christ's sake? No, we can't, a drying rack has to stand on bare rock and not above grass and marshland, which sends fumes and flies and Armageddon up into the fish.

Hans also went into the cowshed, a man in the cowshed.

Martin had never heard or seen anything so ridiculous.

Ingrid began to miss being at home again as she sat on the school bench on Havstein learning arithmetic and reading Bible stories and singing, even though she had friends, whom she missed when she was at home. And during this winter it became abundantly clear to her again, she belonged on Barrøy, an island that no longer had seasons, which was always with her even when she wasn't there.

But if this winter was different, the next summer was too. At the beginning of May Uncle Erling came by with the fishing tackle, the pickings were lean, the season up north had been poor. Likewise, the price they received for their own dried fish at the Trading Post was poor, for here around the islands fishing has been good, claimed Tommesen, the proprietor.

"Tha can row t' Åsværet with tha tiddlers an' see hva tha get thar."

Besides, it wasn't top quality. Tommesen maintained there were too many second-grade fish.

So there were no new buildings on Barrøy that summer. But during June Hans and Martin scraped peat from the bare rock south of the Hammer and moved one drying rack there, so it wasn't quite so far to carry the fish, and the others begin to wonder what this might mean, is Hans planning to be at home for another winter, settle down here, be like them?

Is that even a possibility?

Hans and Maria decide it is, they are free people, they are strong, and together.

But now Hans has no fishing gear to send north with his brother, he needs the rest of the line himself. In addition, they are struggling to get hold of enough bait, herring, small pollack, so throughout January there is more net than line fishing, also on the seaward side of the island. But there the weather is suddenly close on impossible. A lot of the nets Barbro made are lost. She is working her fingers to the bone to make new ones. They too are lost. In February a storm destroys one rack, full of fish. They have to wash them and hang them up again, and Hans wakes in the night more and more often and has to go down to the kitchen and take peeks at the weather and light the fire and pace to and fro and be reminded that he has no coffee, look at the boats and the drying racks, driven by the same disquiet that the stranger left behind, the curious regret. If he had killed him he would never be able to return. He can't see a trace of him now, it is true, but he still won't go away, and Hans wonders if he would have had other spectres in his mind if he had done as he should have done, taken the man's life.

Anxiety can merely be dulled by exhausting work. Now he has both.

The frost arrived and the storm subsided, and fishing was good in the weeks leading up to Easter. Then it turned out to be a year without a spring, one of those years when spring doesn't come until one afternoon at the beginning of June; before then there is just ice and slush, and then cold, slanting rain that has more of a deadening than liberating effect on crops and animals and humans.

Things got so bad that Hans Barrøy began to wonder whether his island was too small, whether these two winters at home had been of any value or whether he had met his destiny, for let's face it, he concluded, first there is one good winter with one good excuse for being at home, then a poor one, of sheer idleness. On top of that, it would take at least another year to remedy the wretched state of affairs, as now he had neither nets nor line. All because of a toe. Two toes. At any rate he wasn't a home-lover any more.

They were building a railway on the mainland, the Nordland Line. It would be the saving of many a poor devil. Now it would be Hans Barrøy's saviour. He was a good ganger and rock-blaster with a sharp eye for the secrets of the mountains. He left for the site as soon as the hay was on the drying racks and didn't come back until the middle of December, hollow-cheeked, straight-backed and as sleepless as a summer's night, but with new equipment, lines, anchor ropes and hooks, bubbling with Lofoten fever more than ever before.

He spent Christmas in the quay house setting up the equipment, eight tubs. And he had brought another novelty with him, as Martin had become so old and Lars was still too young, a windlass, which was installed at the back of the boat shed, so they had something to assist them when the boats had to be pulled in or go out, all you had to do was turn the crank, like on a grindstone.

Maria and Barbro baked and filled another chest of basic provisions for four months, organised his bed linen, clothes . . . and in the small drawer inside: spectacles, razors, camphor drops, pencil, sugar lumps . . . And on January 2 they were there again, seeing off a father and a brother and a husband and an uncle, they waved and shouted to deaf ears while Uncle Erling's aft lantern swung in the winter darkness and it all resembled a funeral. Afterwards they went home and resumed the loneliness and gravity, Barbro, Maria, Ingrid and Lars, a population of four. Martin lay at home in bed on this memorable day, he was only half a man now, ancient and decrepit after the two hardest winters in living memory. In the coming months he would sleep, with a vengeance, may his son stay in Lofoten for a long time, may fortune be with him.

32

Martin had almost stopped working. Before, in the winters, he rowed around the local shores with a jig and some nets, now he was content to do one trip a week, with a trolling line. On these occasions he took Lars with him. Lars was wild and eager. Martin also brought in peat turfs when he had the energy, lit the cod-oil lamps, which no-one else was allowed to touch, saw to the fish and told Barbro how to do this or that, which was neither necessary nor useful. Otherwise he played with little Lars, the Swede, whom he had made his own.

They crawled round on the floor and scrapped. Lars, robust with a strong grip, stood up and pulled his grandfather's hair. Martin thought him too heavy-handed and was equally rough with him. He pretended to be hurt and to want revenge, and the young lad ran out chuckling with laughter. Pursued by his grandfather, all around the island. Until Martin got tired. And he didn't want to play when he was asleep. Karnot, the cat, was still there, she was just as old as Martin and had begun to sleep on his stomach. When he had his midday nap Lars would come in with a wooden stick and poke first the cat, then his grandfather.

"Oh, dammit, A'm not as young as A used t' be," Martin said, got up and went out and looked around to see if there was any work he could do. Usually there wasn't. He chopped up some kindling and showed Lars how to do it.

Ingrid doesn't want to chop wood anymore, she bakes crispbread, *lefse*, bread, she can milk the cows, separate the cream and churn and make *gomme* – sweet cheese and pickle – and spin and knit and row and swim. Ingrid can do almost anything. She can card eider down, arrange nets neatly in the tubs, bait lines, split fish – all men's work – tie fish in pairs for drying – at a pinch women's work – collect gull eggs, pick berries and lift potatoes, strangely enough both men's and women's work. But in the potato field it is like cutting peat, her father stands up and the women are on their knees. Martin is also on his knees. When he isn't lying on his back.

There isn't a twelve-year-old in this world who can do more than Ingrid, she is a daughter of the sea, who doesn't view the crashing waves as a danger or a threat, but as a means and a solution, for most things. One day after her father has left for his labouring job again, she tells Lars that they are going to take the *færing* and row north to Stangholmen, to visit Thomas and Inga, and see if they can get some tobacco for her grandfather, recently Martin has been whingeing so much about not having any tobacco or coffee.

"A got th' money," she says.

She got it from her mother for gilling and salting herring

which they sold at the Trading Post. She has kept it in her chest ever since.

They launch the *færing* into the sea, it is child's play with the new windlass, set the sail and are well over halfway before her mother catches sight of them and comes running out. They pretend they can't hear, her voice is lost in the balmy wind, and they are so near Stangholmen that they can see the houses and crags.

But there is no natural harbour in Stangholmen, only a shallow beach, so they have to sail between some skerries, and as they round the last one and drop sail, Thomas is standing on the shore yelling, just as furiously as Maria.

"Away home wi' tha! Can't tha see the heavens?!"

Pointing to the sky, shaking his head and screaming with rage.

There will be no tobacco or coffee, they don't even row in, but Ingrid doesn't want to go back empty-handed, besides, she can't see anything wrong with the weather, neither can Lars.

They hoist the sail again and cross between the islets towards the Trading Post and they are outside the harbour when the first gust of wind tears the sheets out of Ingrid's hands and threatens to capsize the boat. Lars shouts and narrowly escapes falling overboard. Ingrid turns the stern into the wind, drops sail, almost all of it, and steers dead downward to a green patch on the rock between the Trading Post and the church, Ingrid hasn't set the course but the howling gale and the sea, which is getting rougher and rougher, they are taking in water with every heave, and she screams to Lars that he should go to the bow and jump ashore with the mooring rope before they hit the rock, otherwise he will be sent flying.

They don't meet the rock but the green patch, and the *færing*, with a wet sigh, cuts into a soft cushion of grass and seaweed and comes to a halt with the rudder swinging like a door in the wind.

They climb ashore and try to pull the boat up higher. But it won't budge, and Ingrid knows what is going to happen: the sea will get rougher, the tide will continue to rise and the boat will slowly but surely be smashed to pieces, their precious boat.

And she can't bear to see that.

She drags Lars up the rock with her. Towards the Trading Post. They are soaked from the rain and the sea and no-one can see them crying, not even when they enter the Store and stand in front of Margot, who is serving behind the counter, sturdy Margot, who recognises them and wonders what on earth they are doing out in this weather. She is amazed when she realises they are alone.

"We wan' some tobak f' Grandad," Lars wails.

"Hva kind o' tobak?"

"F' Grandad, f' Grandad . . ."

He is confused, snot runs. Ingrid has to stop herself crying and wipe his nose. He tears himself away and charges outside. She follows and catches up with him in a field where he has come to a standstill, as though his body has seized up, he is shaking and his teeth are chattering.

She leads him back to the Store and they sit on the coke bin and there is nothing they can say. Or do. Now Ingrid can begin to cry again. They are on land, but they want to be on the sea. Then she notices that the wind is dying down, moves out from under the eaves and realises that the rain has let up too, the weather is clearing to the south, the sky is bright.

They go back in, buy rock sugar and a tub of syrup, pay and go without listening to Margot's warnings, run back down to the boat and see it tossing from side to side in the same place, still in one piece.

They bail out the water and push it away on a wave and start rowing.

Ingrid can't believe it.

They row against the swell, each with their two oars, Lars at first in sync with her, then more and more wildly, shouting something, he is counting, she thinks, and he pulls at the oars faster and faster, until she is unable to keep up with him. They are past the last islet. Lars is seasick, has to throw up, and loses an oar, they watch it wave goodbye and disappear. Ingrid rows. Lars goes down on his knees, curls up, lying in the water on the boards with his hands covering his ears. Ingrid is rowing and is hot and has red swirls in front of her eyes, her arms are trembling and her back burning, she rows on and with the last ounce of her strength waits for the final gust of wind, the proof that this will not succeed, because it cannot succeed, it is too far, the sea too frenzied, and the wind picks up, the waves around them are white froth, and she knows they are doomed when a jolt reverberates through the *færing*, it has hit a rock.

But there are no skerries here.

They have collided with another boat.

She turns and sees their big rowing boat. Maria and Barbro at the oars and their grandfather standing up in the huge swell, white, rigid faces and soundless voices, Grandad puts a foot on the railing, waits, sinks, rises, waits and jumps like a youngster into the *færing* and tears the oars out of her hands, pushes her down into the space between the thwarts, where she lies alongside Lars, staring up at him, she watches him drive one oar like a lever into the next swell and turn the *færing* round, so that they have the sea behind them, then he sits down and bends forward with the oars like two black wings raised in the air.

33

When Ingrid awoke she was dead. She was lying on her back in a narrow bed in an empty room and saw light in the window, sun. Yes, indeed. But the bedcover wasn't of down, it was as heavy as lead, and her back ached, her arms trembled and her mind was asleep.

She managed to wriggle onto her right side and saw a white door. A room with a floor, walls and ceiling, all painted white, and a bed, the one she was lying in, and a window, the one she was looking at, a door, which she examined. She wondered if it could be opened, where it led, if she could open it, when a distant noise penetrated all the whiteness, it could have been laughter.

Her name was Ingrid. She was twelve years old, her hair was dry and combed, but not plaited, and lay like a wreath around her head. She held her breath. Exhaled and closed her eyes. Opened them again. Sunlight in the window. No wind, not a sound, the distant voices, the laughter.

She pushed the heavy eiderdown aside and sat up. She could move her limbs, she could struggle up on unsteady legs and stand by the window and look down on a square-shaped meadow which had been grazed to the ground and looked like a green sheet of paper on a brown tabletop. There were some people on it. Two of them were lying back on their elbows, not moving. They were men, who were alive and talking to each other. Two other figures stood some distance away, they were women, they were talking too, though just as soundlessly, and between them a boy with a long stick was running about and drawing a figure of eight on the green sheet. The adults turned and watched him, laughed at him and shouted something.

Ingrid's fingers were claws.

She tried to straighten them. She knew who the people were, her mother and Barbro and her grandfather, the little boy was Lars. And one man was a stranger. Now an unfamiliar woman also came into the picture. The others turned and smiled at her. She gave them small white cups, filled them from a jug, they drank and talked, and Ingrid now recognised Stangholmen, the man was Thomas, and the woman was Inga. Ingrid had been here before, a handful of times, but they had often waved to each other across the water. When she raised her eyes she could make out Barrøy in the distance.

She was on the wrong side of the sea.

The bad: she was able to straighten her claws and saw that the knuckles were red and chafed. She looked down at her knees protruding from under the edge of her skirt and the blood that ran in a thin line over her kneecap and down her calf, another stream down the inside of her other knee. She opened her mouth to scream and heard nothing. Down on the green sheet of paper everyone froze and stared up at her, she saw her mother open her mouth, close it again and start running towards her.

The good: they rowed home together, Maria and Ingrid in the *færing*, Barbro and Lars, each taking an oar in the rowing boat. Martin sat on the aft thwart laughing at them, pointing out all the things they couldn't do, above all else row properly. The sea was calm with a long, lazy swell. It was October. They competed to get home first. Her mother had explained to her about the blood. Ingrid was told not to row harder than Maria. Lars and Barbro came first. Lars cheered. The cows were bellowing in the barn. The sheep lay in the Garden of Eden eating potato haulms. From the roof of the quay house an eagle alighted. From one drying rack, another. But blood had flowed. And when Ingrid turned she could see Thomas and Inga like small chess pieces on Stangholmen's southernmost headland.

"Nu tha can wave t'em," Ingrid's mother said, winding in the *færing*. "So they ca' see we're heim."

Ingrid went to the top of the crag and waved, thinking of everything she would have to forget, the man who came and stole something they didn't know they had. And on the other island they waved back with a green scarf, they called it the signal scarf. They also had a red one, which they used when they needed help. Behind her, Maria said she should go with her to the cowshed while Barbro cooked dinner. She also asked:

"Hva's this hier?"

A brown lump on the floor of the *færing*. The rock sugar. But the tub of syrup was still intact. Ingrid lifted it up, weighed it in both hands and could feel how important it was, the weight of it, it was undamaged, and she carried it up to the house.

34

Nelly is visiting. It is Easter, Good Friday and low, low tide, the short period of the year when the island is at its biggest and they can walk on snow-white sand around the whole kingdom, apart from below the Hammer and the new quay, where the water is always so deep that Lars can dive into it, the others don't. But Ingrid has once swum all the way around the island, at high tide, when the island was at its smallest, that was in the middle of a hotter summer than all the others.

Now she does the round with Nelly, who is here because her mother is visiting family. Nothing is said about her father, nor her siblings.

Nelly asks questions that have never been asked on Barrøy: Why don't you have any keyholes in doors? Who is Lars's father? Why haven't you got any brothers or sisters? What does your grandfather say to that?

Ingrid knows which questions she mustn't ask her mother. But she ruminates on the most important one, reviews it continually, the question of why she is an only child, children on other islands have nine or even thirteen siblings. Nelly has six brothers, and on Stangholmen Thomas and Inga raised five girls and three boys, who left one by one when they had finished school and now are only there to help in the busy season, otherwise the two parents are alone, they have been alone for as long as Ingrid can remember.

But they have two scarves to signal with, one green, the other red.

Nelly also has a few criticisms of Barrøy: first of all, there is no-one else here, not like on her island of Lauøy, where there are four whole families. And aren't there any dogs here? And the houses aren't painted. Nelly's house isn't painted either, but one building which doesn't belong to her family is red, it is the only building they can see from the school on Havstein, Nelly can point it out, her neighbour's barn.

Nelly is not too keen on boiled pollack or liver, either. But she is obviously exaggerating because she eats as heartily as Lars. And there is a lot of food she likes, whether she says so or not: cinnamon biscuits with butter, last year's rhubarb jam, fresh milk, crispbread, the eiderdown she sleeps under beside Ingrid in the North Chamber, they don't have down on Lauøy. She also appreciates having her own chair, which she sits on at meal times. It is Hans's chair, he is in Lofoten as usual, so she sits at the head of the table, like a queen, and she probably hasn't sat there very often, looking straight at Martin, who sits at the other end. And walking around a whole island at low tide, like on the brim of an enormous hat, and collecting gulls' eggs in small net baskets, you can't do that on every island.

In addition, Nelly is a good worker, even though Maria says

they should take time off and do what they want, which is also something new for Ingrid.

Nelly has plaited her hair, which swings between her shoulders like a rope when they tease Lars, making him run after them across the sand dunes. Lars is a stocky lad, and hot-tempered, but not very tall. They throw eggs at him, the yolks run like gleaming honey down his furious face. Ingrid enjoys being naughty. And Lars is stupid enough to wipe himself down in the dry heather and looks like a lumpsucker when he comes home. Ingrid is given a bigger tongue-lashing than she has ever had before, those precious eggs. But Nelly gets the same treatment. While Lars takes a run-up and punches Ingrid in the face, so hard that Maria has to stuff rags up her nostrils to staunch the blood.

Problems arise with Martin too, such as when he can't sleep, he walks around and feels like a stranger in his own world, since Lars only runs after the girls.

On top of that, he is grumpy, and talks in a mumble, that is why Nelly asks what he is saying, this too is a question there is no answer to, even if Ingrid understands everything he says, also everything he doesn't say.

But what about her not having any brothers or sisters?

At the beginning Nelly says she is homesick. But as the day for her return approaches she starts to sob and expels short bursts of air through her nostrils. Maria says that Barbro and Ingrid don't need to go to the cowshed with them, Nelly is enough, and talks to her in private. And when they emerge

Nelly is almost like she was when she arrived, although she still doesn't want to go home, she wants to live on Barrøy for the rest of her life, it is the best place she has ever been.

Over dinner, Martin asks if she has been to that many places.

Nelly says she has been to both Havstein and Lauøy, and once to the Trading Post with her father, but actually they deliver their catches to another trading post, in Åsværet, and she has never been there.

Martin laughs. Nelly does too. He asks her what her grandfather's name is, and it transpires that Martin fished with him for many winters, in Træna. So he asks more questions, which Nelly understands and answers.

Then Lars also asks a question, how many brothers has she got?

She counts up the whole impressive collection, and Lars asks yet another question, to Barbro this time, why hasn't he got any brothers?

And there is a silence.

Lars glances at Ingrid, from her to Maria, and his eyes stop there, he is thinking so hard they can hear the cogs creaking, then he opens his mouth as Martin gets to his feet and says, well, he has to go out and see to the calf that was given soot yesterday, it has a bad stomach, and Ingrid asks Lars if he wants another egg in his face.

Everyone laughs at that, except Lars.

He gets up and follows his grandfather.

*

After they have gone to bed, Ingrid hears Nelly sniffling in her sleep and mumbling words she doesn't understand. But she feels a deep gratitude at being able to hear the unconscious groans of someone who doesn't ever want to leave Barrøy and who used to plait her hair when it hung down to her waist.

Maria and Barbro row them back.

Ingrid is sitting in her best clothes, with a sore nose, next to Nelly and watching her grandfather and Lars on the Hammer at home, an old man and a little lad on her island, which is becoming smaller and smaller, while Nelly sobs and coughs and makes no attempt to hide her tears, as though she can at last cry to her heart's content and doesn't want to miss the chance to make up for lost time. When they arrive on Havstein she is pale and composed. The girls walk up to the Farm and turn and wave to Maria and Barbro, who are already clear of the harbour. Barbro raises an oar and waves back. Ingrid is at home both here and there. She is a sentimental child. And very happy.

35

More than a year passes before the opportunity presents itself to have the question of brothers and sisters cleared up; this type of thing just doesn't go away.

It is a murderously hot summer, the hottest in living memory. The sky and sea merge in a thick stew that hangs over them day and night and scorches and stunts the grass and makes the potato plants go limp while the animals and humans sweat and pant. They walk around semi-naked in the swarms of flies on a tropical island by the Arctic Circle.

Hans moves the stove in the Swedes' boathouse onto the crag because it is impossible to cook indoors anymore. They sleep with the windows and doors open and bathe every day. In the sea. Even old Martin has a dip, he wades through the water, like Hans and Barbro, while Lars dives from the rocks and Maria and Ingrid swim over to Moltholmen and sit on the smooth rocks in the sun and close their eyes and think about nothing until they swim back.

Barrøy is a paradise.

But by the beginning of July the new rainwater tank is empty. Then the peat bogs dry out, one by one, after that the rock pools on Skogsholmen, this is becoming ridiculous. And as there is no wind, Hans and Martin have to row when they go to the Trading Post with their empty churns and buckets. But they have run out of water there as well. They have to go to the mountain stream by Malvika, how wonderful it would have been with some wind in their sails, here where at all other times there was never anything but.

They do two trips a day, after which their backs ache so much that they can manage no more. Humans don't drink much, but they drink more than usual, and the animals can't get enough.

Then the last patches of snow on the mountains disappear, the stream by Malvika dries up, the gulls don't take off anymore, only waddle away when Lars chases them, and otherwise bob up and down on the sluggish sea that has become a desert.

Hans conducts hushed conversations with Maria, will they have to slaughter some animals?

Maria hedges, this is a question for a man, and for him to answer. And driven by a desperate impulse, he equips his family with pickaxes and spades, they have to start digging, at the bottom of the old well in the bog, which is also dry.

Hans and Lars are down a black hole cursing and fighting off flies and clegs while the others pull up bucket after bucket of rust-red soil and spread it over hollows in fields and meadows. They are born of the soil and tied to it with indestructible bonds, but now it is not only under their nails and soles but in their pores and thoughts, in their ears, hair and eyes, the last area it conquers is the patch in the centre of their backs where frantic hands cannot reach in their hysterical battle with clegs and gadflies.

But they can wash in a sea which for once is warm, their bodies give off brown clouds, which they swim away from, white and new-born, licking salt from their lips before they go up again to engage with the well. Even an island has to have ground water, it doesn't flow like a ship of course, but is moored to the earth's core, Hans has said it before, and water is down there, it has to be.

A kind of desperation has entered his life, worry is written in the whites of his eyes, this is dangerous, a danger so unnatural it has not been possible to predict, when was there last such a summer as this?

Was it this that wiped out the civilisation in Karvika?

A drought?

Out here?

One afternoon they hear a distant scream from Lars deep down in the shaft, and the next bucket is full of mud, wet sludge.

If they were covered in soil before, it was nothing compared with now. Lars and Hans strip off and work naked in the hole like a pair of stokers in a scene from the Bible, wet echoes of their curses resound, and when they climb up the ladder for a break the others can't tell the difference between the two of them, except by their height.

"Hvur's it goen' then?"

"Ya-a . . ."

When they walk back, nice and clean after the next wash, Hans suddenly stops in the meadow and says shh and puts a hand to his ear, he has heard something, the sound of water. His eyes trickle as well, and the others have to look away. He sets off at a run, they follow him and lie down in a circle around the gunshot wound in the island and stare down at a stygian eye staring furiously back at them, they don't make a sound.

The water smells of fart and marsh and oil, but there is no rainbow reflection in it. Hans orders bits of old bed linen to be stretched over barrels and buckets, to act as a sieve. They can see the bottom of the first bucket already. They give this water to the cows, which are standing around them gasping. The water in the next one is clearer, the trickling sound hasn't become less faint but more pronounced, like a gurgling stream. And the following morning they are busy setting up a hoisting contraption over the well hole, a five-legged tepee of poles with a block and tackle and ropes and beneath it dangles a board which Lars can sit on. They lower him carefully, he scoops one full bucket of water after the other from the surface, they winch them up and give them to the animals, which moo and bleat, now the sheep have also flocked around them, panicky and relieved at the same time. They can make coffee with the water. By evening they can also drink it as it comes, it is icy cold and tastes of nothing.

That same night they watered the potato field. The following morning it was as dry as before, but the haulms were now up to their knees. They hoisted Lars up and down, he scooped and scooped, they watered the potatoes all day long and also the next night, the water pearled in the dusty furrows and evaporated, but the grass became even more erect. And so a week passed.

Then the rains came.

And hit them with the sensation of having gone through a week like no other, seven sacred days from when they found water beneath their own feet to the heavens opening above them. Rich, despairing days, the final proof that they themselves rule over their destinies. The island had been brown like a November day from the beginning of June to the end of July. Now it was greener than ever, even Rose Acre was no longer red. Then came sunshine and rain in turn, and they had a meagre hay crop. The harvest on the islets was poor, too, but it is still better to slaughter animals before Christmas than in the middle of summer. And one afternoon Ingrid, lying on her back beside her mother in the freshly mown Scab Acre, realised they had survived and the critical question could be asked, in a new atmosphere of freedom, why didn't she have any brothers or sisters?

Maria raised herself onto her elbows and said that children are not something you have, you are given them, they are gifts. Ingrid asked why some are given children and others are not, although something told her she ought to keep quiet.

"Has tha missed haven' someone?" her mother asked in a sharp tone. But immediately changed tack and asked if Ingrid remembered when Nelly had been here the previous year, how Nelly had cried when she had to return home, that was because

165

they hadn't teased her on Barrøy when she stammered, not even Lars had, Nelly could thank Maria for that, just so that Ingrid didn't go getting any ideas.

Ingrid looked at her, in puzzlement.

"She's got brothers 'n' sisters," Maria said pointedly. And Ingrid wanted to ask what she meant by that, as though she wished to hear it all again, that being on your own had some value, but a shadow had crossed her face, it was Lars, who had crept up on them soundlessly and was blocking the sun. Maria peered up and asked where Grandad was.

"He's haven' a nap," the boy said.

His trousers were too big, Barbro had cut off the legs, they were held up by braces she had plaited with float line, he walked around like that all day, barefoot, semi-naked and wild, he had the body of an adult, was seven years old and about to start school.

"Hvar?" Maria asked.

"Thar," said the boy, pointing in a direction that made her look towards a part of the island where Martin never went, where no-one went, over by Karvika and the ruins. But her eyes didn't find what they were looking for, so she got up, brushed grass off her skirt and kept searching, until a little cry escaped from her mouth and she broke into a run. Ingrid and Lars stared at her in astonishment.

36

Martin, a man who could not get enough of the sun, had stretched out in the shade to rest, he seemed to be sleeping as he always slept, all that was missing was Karnot, the cat, on his belly.

Maria turned and stopped the children, spotted her husband, who had put down his scythe and was walking towards them at a leisurely pace. From the house came Barbro, not knowing what to expect, they all came, as if at a signal.

Hans squatted down on his haunches at his father's side and laid a hand on Martin's cheek. Nobody said anything. He straightened up, fixed his gaze on Lars and said he should go with him to fetch something from the quay house. Ingrid heard them talking, Lars eagerly, her father explaining something, she couldn't hear what.

They returned with the ladder they had used when constructing the rainwater tank and two of the rugs the Swedes had slept on. Hans placed one of them over the ladder. He and Barbro lifted their father onto it, spread the other rug over him, carried the ladder to the boat shed and lowered it onto the rollers where the *færing* usually rested. After that they closed both doors and also the opening at the back so no birds could get at him.

Next morning they left for the mainland in two boats. Barbro and Hans rowed the larger of the two *færings*. Ingrid and Maria sat in the stern. Lars was in the forepeak, crying his eyes out. In tow they had a rowing boat carrying Martin on the ladder, there was no wind.

They put in at the small landing stage beneath the Trading Post. Hans went up and came back with Pastor Johannes Malmberget, who had to have assistance climbing down the steep steps. He took their hands in his, one by one, and spoke the soothing words he had uttered so many times, though he still managed to make them sound sincere. The steamer had just delivered ice, so they could put the body in cold storage.

"Has tha minded th' clout?"

Yes, they had remembered to bring a bundle of clothes with them, Martin's Sunday best.

What about the coffin?

Yes, they had the money.

Hans and Barbro carried the ladder bearing their father up the steps and into the cold-storage room and put it down on two trestles between towering stacks of ice blocks covered in sawdust, which had been cut out of a lake last winter and had even survived the warmest summer in living memory, it was comforting and cold in there, and so quiet you could hear the drips.

They went back out, onto the wharf, where a handful of

people had collected in the sunshine. One of the Trading Post workers came and shook Hans by the hand and said something he wasn't intended to hear. He also shook Barbro's hand. The funeral was discussed. Pastor Malmberget apologised for not accompanying them down the steep steps. Hans said it didn't matter. They shook hands once again and went down to the *færing* and rowed back home with the other boat in tow.

Karnot the cat and Lars mourned most. Lars howled and smashed everything in his path. Hans was silent. Barbro quietly wept when she thought nobody was watching. Maria's face was stiff and pallid, like the time she feared they were going to lose the animals in the drought. And Ingrid discovered that some grief is more heartfelt than other grief, above all hers. She went to the Hammer near the quay house hoping a large hand would sweep her into the sea and hold her beneath the waves until she died, as she didn't have the strength to jump, and she couldn't go to pieces on land either, even though she was sobbing with all her heart, until Maria came and tore her away from the edge of the crag and told her to pull herself together, now maybe she understood what she had done when she went away with Lars in the *færing*, Martin was an old man, children are children, there is an ocean of difference.

Ingrid twisted and squirmed away and became a snake and then a hard, silent knot. She was allowed to sleep next to her mother in the North Chamber, while her father lay alone in the South Chamber, and before her eyes closed, that old burning sensation was back, in her stomach, from the time when she wondered whether she could trust her father or her mother, or indeed anyone at all.

The day the funeral was to take place Uncle Erling docked at the new quay. With his boat full of relatives Ingrid had heard a lot about, but only seen a few of, her father's four sisters, with their husbands, her mother's three younger sisters, with two spouses, Uncle Erling and his wife Helga with her elderly father as well as all fifteen brothers and sisters of widely different ages, picked up from various islands and islets over the last twenty-four hours and sailed here, to Barrøy, to collect the remaining few.

They climbed aboard and shook hands and greeted left, right and centre without a word being spoken, then a massive calm descended over this ark chugging over towards the Trading Post in the continuing sunshine.

They shouted for a gangway and stood for a few moments witnessing a ship being securely moored before they moved off in a body, performing an unsteady jig, and made their way up to the Store and the houses, to the most windswept parish in all of the Lord's Realm of Horrors, clad in their glittering black finery, a slow march to the church, where everything proceeded as it should with Pastor Johannes Malmberget at the helm, accompanied by his comely wife and two small sons, plus Thomas and Inga from Stangholmen, who had come over by oar power, as usual, and about a dozen other islanders, more people than Ingrid had ever had around her, all of them deferentially nodding at Malmberget's well-chosen words about Martin's forty-three winters in an open boat on the sea around Træna, that was why he had such coarse hands. With a life like that it was only by the grace of God that they had a body to commit to the earth, although the sea is also a heaven, we must never lose sight of this fact, especially not out here, nor should we forget that the old man passed away so peacefully, at the place where he would have wished to pass away, Martin Konrad Hansen Barrøy, on his own island, finally resting here beside his beloved Kaja, his somewhat prematurely departed wife, a storm-battered yearning has at long last come to fruition, that is how we have to look upon it as we stand here with quivering lips and our tears at high tide, sighed Johannes Malmberget, wiping the sweat from his scalp with a red handkerchief, where-after he raised his eyes to behold the craggy mountains and give the sexton the sign to start lowering the coffin into what, in Ingrid's eyes, looked alarmingly like the well they had dug a good month ago, amen, it was unbearable.

On the way back to the island Hans remembered something, grabbed the wheel from his brother's hands and turned back to fetch the ladder and two rugs they had left lying on the wharf outside the cold-storage room, it was as good as new, that ladder.

Ingrid was speechless.

Not that she had said so much previously that day. And the priest's sober words were further undermined by a noticeable

171

change in the mood on board, the peace and calm of the church-yard was supposed to be eternal, wasn't it, even the wind held its breath, but now laughter could be heard by the hold cover, by the port railing one of Ingrid's aunts was hugging Maria, who was holding her hand to her mouth to stop herself laughing too. The smallest children had begun to run wild around the deck, unchecked by their elders. And through the window in the wheelhouse Ingrid could see a bottle of spirits balancing on the compass, the only perpendicular object in the heavy swell, as well as five green glasses which passed from hand to hand between her father and his companions.

They moored the boat on Barrøy, the hold hatch was thrown open and crates of food and drink hoisted ashore, bed linen and clothes. And a swarm of strangers surged in over the island rediscovering its every long-forgotten nook and cranny.

"Does tha mind th' North Wind Ridge?"

"Thar's Kvitsanda . . ."

The crags, the meadows, the coves . . . there was not an inch of this island these strangers didn't know like the back of their hands and were overjoyed to see again. Ingrid was no longer a resident of her own island, with all her insights into its treasures and secrets, but a dumbstruck visitor to the lives of others, as they once had been and always would be, for no childhood can be erased.

One of her father's sisters fell to her knees and dug up an overgrown eider-duck house, which Ingrid had never seen, then she found another, which Ingrid knew nothing about either, cleaned it up and wanted some slate tiles to mend it, Ingrid was told where she could find some. The guests didn't need to be shown anything, they knew where the down was and where the fishing grounds were, where the eagles nested, all the shelves and secret drawers of the island's larder. Even the children who had never been here before had an irritating tendency to feel at home, went into the boat shed and quay house and rooted around, two boys launched the rowing boat without so much as a by-your-leave and took Lars with them, he was whooping with glee and pointing this way and that and had forgotten what day it was, the best day of his life, while the girls stood on dry land like tiny black tents and didn't want to join in, they just stared and acted as though they were sisters, presumably because their own islands lay close together, Ingrid's was more remote.

But a girl of Ingrid's age was standing in front of her, look-ing at Ingrid with a sorrowful countenance beneath dark, heavy eyebrows, she also said something, but again came the sound of Maria's laughter as she and her sister-in-law set about clearing Grandad's room so they could scrub it and remove all traces.

"Is tha Ingrid?"

Ingrid nodded, it was too early to say anything.

"A'm Josefine, fro' Gåsværet."

Ingrid nodded again and spotted Karnot darting between the unfamiliar legs, having been banished from her own home, which she had refused to leave since Martin's death, now she scuttled down to the boat shed, looking as if she was planning to take to the water.

On the beach her father and Uncle Erling had lit a bonfire. The old rugs went up in flames. One of her aunts came with a bundle of old clothes, then her mother with Grandad's bedclothes, the sparks rose skyward on the golden August day, there was Barbro with Martin's palliasse, she had become the robust baby sister in a seven-strong bevy of siblings, who was hugged and pampered and teased, she beamed like the sun and had her hair combed in various styles as she sat on her chair in the open air like a queen. She no longer sat alone, either, all the chairs were outside, the parlour and kitchen tables too, there was coffee and food and cakes and spirits, those that didn't have a chair lay on rugs or in the grass and ate and drank, enveloped in the buzz of voices and laughter and everything else that belongs to life and not to death.

Ingrid wanted to go to the Hammer and be swept into the sea again. But there was no escaping her cousin Josefine's stolid gaze. Now too she felt her muscles contract into an involuntary smile when one of her uncles fell flat on his face to the joyous applause of the others. She shed a few tears, but her smile held and she answered all the questions until night fell like gentle rain upon the infinite crowd of people that had transformed Barrøy into a town, a foreign town, it was enough to drive you crazy, and behind it all she constantly saw her mother as she had never seen her before. She didn't understand her. It was as strange a sensation as feeling sorry for a grandfather.

37

It is a year and a day since the new quay on Barrøy was completed. Hans Barrøy has not only regarded it as a triumph and an architectural masterpiece but also felt obliged to continue the good work. He has also written several important letters and been to meetings with the Department of Transport and the dairy and the local council regarding his projects.

To no avail.

But after his father's death he has to make another attempt, and this time he takes Maria with him to the mainland. The three left standing on the beach watching them disappear in light drizzle think something momentous is afoot.

This is all about adding Barrøy to the milk route, which runs three times a week between the Trading Post and Havstein and two other islands, picking up milk churns, and which in emergencies also functions as a passenger ferry for the inhabitants of the islands, even if it is no more than a condemned fishing smack, moreover it alleviates all the hassle of getting the bull to the cows or the cows to the bull. Hans has also taken along a chart, which he unrolls on the chief administrative officer's kitchen table to show him that a stop in Barrøy would not be much of a detour.

But they are only met with more non-committal goodwill and some words about the local council budget, which has never been tighter, besides the admin officer has nothing to do with this case, he claims.

Maria notices that no coffee is served, and that has nothing to do with the budget, and the conversation treads water for a while until it suddenly acquires a philosophical dimension, the admin officer remembers that for years Hans Barrøy has sabotaged the civilised world's need for a seamark, a lamp or a beacon that ships can use to navigate, on Barrøy or one of its close-lying islets or skerries, after all his property lies right in the middle of the fairway, or more precisely, on its seaward side.

Hans asks what this has to do with his case and is told that the admin officer has had an idea, perhaps they can strike an informal deal, you see, his son works for the Lighthouse Authorities, so what about three calls a week on the milk route in exchange for them being allowed to set up a beacon on, shall we say, Skarvholmen, what does Hans Barrøy say to that, to this rock being of use for once instead of just a skerry in the sea?

He doesn't know what to think.

It ruins his sleep.

He would rather have a cairn than a light. But he would prefer not to have either, not to sit at the kitchen window staring at a black finger pointing up on his horizon, probably with a white belt around its middle and an iron pennant on top. And then there are the works that would have to be carried out, it would be months of people and coming and going. And how many cows will he be able to feed if he, for example, reclaims the marshland on Gjesøya, which is close to Barrøy, to grow more grass, it should have been done generations ago, and thirdly: when it comes down to it, does he really want this boat coming three times a week?

In other words the question is turned more and more on its head as the threat of getting what he wants looms closer by the day.

All of this is bound up with his father's death.

With the island's continued existence.

One year has passed already, and some years are longer than others, he ties his body in knots and tosses his head, comes to a final decision and lets Maria pen the next letter, her handwriting is neater and she has a number of other linguistic merits. They sail to the mainland and deliver it together, again to the chief administrative officer, with a copy for the dairy, they are given a verbal assurance on the spot, and travel back home, Christ, that was quick, they are almost giggling on the way home, two youngsters who have opened themselves to the world, they have become a name on the map, they are visible.

But when, two weeks later, the milk route makes its first call and all five of them are standing on the quay, where they grab the hawser – one is enough because the boat is only going to take one milk churn on board, and that is so little that the skipper, with whom Hans went to school, smiles condescend-ingly at both the freshly painted number on the churn and the fact that this was the cause of all the fuss, the other islands supply between ten and twenty – then Hans Barrøy realises that he has made a pact with the Devil, there was no going back, he will immediately have to reclaim Gjesøya, there is no way round it.

He drops the railway job that autumn and rows Lars, who in fact should have started school, to Gjesøya and they set about digging drains. With a pickaxe and a spade. They make sure there is a fall and put rocks and brushwood in the trenches, there could be some big pastures here between the crags.

But it is a colossal task, it is soul- and body-destroying, and after only two weeks Hans begins to doubt whether this is at all feasible. Not that he has any thoughts of giving up so soon. Barbro joins them for a few weeks, she is a dab hand with a spade. After another month they hire two unemployed youths from the main island. But they have to be paid, with money the islanders don't have.

When the frost finally comes, Hans Barrøy straightens his back and conducts a crucial conversation with himself: this new land lying in front of him, which he can contemplate with weary satisfaction, it is indescribably beautiful, no doubt about that, but is it actually his, in the same way as the other fields and pastures?

It is almost a macabre thought, which indicates that he doesn't like working with the soil, he is a man of the sea, more a fisherman than a farmer, more a hunter than a slave of the earth. What was once intended to be no more than a slightly extravagant extra piece of land is in the process of becoming an existential abscess.

There has always been a conflict inside him between sea and land, in the form of a restlessness and an attraction: when he is at sea he longs to be at home and if he has his fingers in the soil he always catches himself staring at the sea and thinking about fishing. But there has been a balance in this toing and froing, an acceptable interdependence, which is now under threat.

He can't resolve his confusion, instead he goes over to Lars and tells him to forget the bloody brushwood he is toiling and moiling with, they are calling it a day, for this year.

They gather up their tools and row home in the silence that always descends on them when Lars cannot bring himself to ask what is going on and Hans pretends he doesn't understand what the boy wants to know, this time he doesn't know himself, it is a natural silence. The two youths are paid and leave that same afternoon on the milk run. With one churn of milk.

There it is again:

Barrøy gets cheese in return for this milk.

As well as butter, cream and sour cream, which they used to produce themselves. Well, they still do, with the milk they keep, but is this progress? They need cash, for fishing equipment and boats and everything to do with the sea, not the same cheese that has been made elsewhere, by other people.

He has never felt more wretched.

But it is December now, the time of year when decisions can be postponed. He fishes along the seaward side of the island with Lars until Christmas and gradually reaches some kind of clarity about the situation. After another winter in Lofoten he comes home and goes to buy timber, four oil drums and a hundred running metres of solid planks so that they can build a raft south of Barrøy and float animals across the sound to Gjesøya, this is done on many other islands.

So Gjesøya will not be used for growing hay but grazing. For calves. While the cows can stay at home. Now they can produce more milk. And raise more young animals.

When Lars starts school he arrives at Havstein on his first day accompanied by Maria and Barbro, not rowing but sitting on one of Barrøy's two churns on board the milk run. He is still short, so no-one makes any fuss about him starting a year late. He is quick on the uptake as well, and he can read. And, at home on Barrøy, Hans feels once again that he has wasted a year.

Nevertheless, it has been an important year. Much more important than the two previous ones he wasted. Even if he still isn't clear in his mind how much more. He misses his father.

38

That same autumn the cairn is to be put up. But it is done in Hans Barrøy's absence, for now he has to take a labouring job again, the railway and cash. It is also done in Ingrid's absence, she is to be confirmed and have preparatory classes with fifteen other young people from the islands, she will be staying with Karen Louise Malmberget for the duration, and be looking after the priest's two sons when she isn't studying, learning how to be a maidservant, moreover together with Nelly and Josefine and another girl, does it get any better than that? What is more, Karen Louise is pregnant again, it will be the priest's eighth child, and none of them has died.

This means that only Maria and Barbro are on Barrøy when the Lighthouse Authorities arrive. The workforce consists of eleven men, they have their own boats and rafts, and are dressed like a mixture of labourers and foremen, a superior class of worker, with cloth caps, waistcoats, shiny bucket boots and woollen sweaters which make them look like engineers. They are well-mannered and polite when they want to buy meat or fish or crispbread, and also spend quite a lot of money. They sleep on board an iron-reinforced boat by the name of

Glunten II, which is moored at the new quay when it can't anchor right by their workplace, which it does in good weather.

But there is a misunderstanding on the very first day, which Maria doesn't clear up, or else she doesn't care. They don't start work on Skarvholmen, as agreed, but on the southern tip of Barrøy itself. It isn't a cairn either but an iron construction, four upright T-beams are driven down and cemented firmly into the rock and they support a lantern on top, about six feet high, a white lighthouse with a red hat which from a distance looks like an insect or a circus clown hovering in the air. It will be fired by paraffin, which is drawn up via a pipe from a tank bolted to the rock beneath, and it will burn from October 1 to March 1, and be turned off – though easily visible with its red and white colours – for the rest of the year.

Now it will soon be November.

So there has been a pulsating light on Barrøy's southern-most tip for more than a month when the navvy comes home and hits the roof, a permanent garish Christmas tree on his island!

But he is not met by any sympathy, neither from Maria nor Barbro. They show him one hundred and twenty-two kroner, which they have received as ground rent and tell him that for the rest of their lives they will also receive a small though regular income for looking after and maintaining the light. They have become not only milk producers and a name on the map but lighthouse keepers and wage earners, in the service of the state.

Hans Barrøy can't stomach this.

He is not going to be in anyone's service.

He goes on the milk run to the mainland the next day, without Maria. And even before Barrøy fades into the sea behind him, he considers the fact that he isn't rowing or sailing but making his entrance on a new route, wearing his best clothes, as though there is some weakness in the complaint he is planning to lodge and this unorthodox "deal" they have entered into, perhaps it is not as easy to complain after all, and to which authority?

He stands in the wheelhouse with his old school friend, Paulus, who has had this cushy job for decades, a fixed income for doing nothing more than sailing in safe waters between the Trading Post and the islands and taking shore leave whenever he wants.

In Havstein Hans helps to take the milk on board, all twenty-one churns from the five farms, which they lower into the hold and secure to ballast blocks before continuing to Skarven, where they take on fifteen more, and another eleven at Lutvær, before arriving at the Trading Post late that evening. By then it is too late to sail over to the mainland to visit the admin officer, so he goes straight to the fishermen's shack which is there for all island folk, lights the stove, makes coffee and sleeps on the matter.

He doesn't go up to the houses the next morning either. The steamer, the island's connection with the mainland, is moored at the Trading Post wharf. And something stirs in him. He goes on board and sails to the town, goes to the fishing-supplies

183

store and purchases four new line tubs, eight coils of rope, buoy line, hooks, hemp yarn and knives. Then he buys coffee, a sack of sugar, a sack of peas and a bucket of smoked sausages, a Christmas tablecloth, three Christmas magazines for children, two bottles of aquavit, eight metres of blue-flowered dress material and a dresser with six drawers plus a framed picture of a sailing ship.

He takes the steamer back the same afternoon, spends the night in the fishermen's shack, carries his purchases to the milk-route boat and is home on Barrøy exactly two days after he left.

He is received there by his family, who are standing on the quay with two churns.

The dresser doesn't make the greatest impression on them, what interests them are the Christmas magazines and the tablecloth. But that is before they take a closer look at the piece of furniture and see how perfectly it fits into the parlour. Maria can see that something isn't quite right about all this. She opens the drawers, they glide like oiled wheels on greased rails, it has inward-curving legs with tiny cat's paws, carvings on the front of all the drawers and four rounded corners, and on a brass plate at the back she reads: KOFOED & SON, CABINETMAKERS, NIDAROS.

She asks her husband what on earth he was thinking of. Doesn't she think it is wonderful, he says. She wants to know how much it cost. He says he can't remember. She asks him if he got a receipt. He says no. She pulls out the drawers and pushes them back in and catches a fragrance of camphor and hibiscus

184

and cherry, she doesn't know what it is, she recognises the scent of something exotic and looks at the man with his back to her, holding a hammer and nails, hanging up the picture of the sailing ship beside the east-facing window. He makes sure it is straight, goes to the kitchen and sits down in his father's rocking chair, then pours himself a dram and lights his pipe and says that tomorrow they are going to slaughter the pig. They haven't always had pigs on Barrøy, but this year they have one. Tomorrow it is going to die.

Across the table sit Ingrid and Lars reading their Christmas magazines. Barbro is reading one too, it has pictures. Maria gets started on the dinner. They eat, drink coffee, and Barbro tells Lars to write some Christmas cards to their relatives on Buøy and Gjesværet, which they can send via the milk run. She is mute with admiration at his handwriting.

When the children have gone to bed Hans pours three more drams and gives Maria and Barbro one each and pushes the one hundred and twenty-two kroner back across the table so that this winter they won't have to go shopping on the slate while he is in Lofoten. Maria says it isn't necessary. He says, yes, it is. She says that actually he doesn't have this money to give. He loses his temper, jumps up and goes to bed. The money is still on the table. Then Maria gets up too and goes to bed. Barbro hears voices in the South Chamber. Then silence. She knocks back her dram, and Maria's, stokes up the stove and takes the money with her up to her room. Barbro has a chest, too.

39

After confirmation classes at the rectory on the main island, Ingrid thinks Barrøy is boring. It doesn't help that there is a light there to guide ships through the darkness. Not that she yearns to leave, what she yearns for is a different Barrøy, or she would like to take the island with her into the outside world and fill it with everything it lacks, and this everything amounts to quite a lot, bursting as she is with her yearnings, for it is a grind to fetch peat and go to the cowshed and potato cellar and pull in the nets with Barbro and gut fish, this is not something real women do, they stand in front of mirrors and sing in choirs and wait for a letter to arrive, they laugh with other women and go for walks in groups wearing the same clothes, beneath an azure sky where the sea cannot be heard, not even in the distance.

Strangely enough, even less happens on Barrøy in the following winters, the nights are so sleepless that she wonders whether she is ill, and stays in bed until her mother forces her to get up, she has nobody to love here, Barrøy is unrecognisable with the monotonous murmur of the water and the wind, which she never noticed before, it is driving her insane, as is the screeching and squawking of the gulls, the oystercatchers and the eiders and the stupid cormorants, which stand like coal-black monks out on the skerry and turn their cowls to catch the wind, she will have to leave to work as a maid, she will.

But the world doesn't want her.

Suddenly the world has acquired a surplus of people like Ingrid. Maria searches and enquires, both with and without her daughter's knowledge, but it is as it is, and her father says she can go with him to Lofoten as a cook. But Maria won't have any of this, she has been a cook in Lofoten herself, that was where she met Hans, that is enough. And it is even more difficult when Lars is at home and wants Ingrid to go fishing with him and she has become far too much of a woman. She goes nonetheless and rests on her oars while Lars stands legs akimbo pulling in the nets and bleeding the fish in a crazed fury, in the hell where he belongs.

But one day Maria shows her the letter at last, where it says that she has got a placement, with Oskar Tommesen, the son of the owner of the Trading Post, and his young wife Zezenie, who is from somewhere in the south of the country, they have two children who are to be taken care of in a newly built house opposite the Post.

"Tha should a left years back."

Ingrid nods.

"It'll be ne'er s' hard nu tho'," says Maria, as if she is aware that all roads lead home. Or perhaps it is envy. Or the nascent sense of loss. But the milk route has become a clock, it has brought them into line with the time system on the mainland.

*

Fru Tommesen and her children are waiting as Ingrid steps ashore at the Trading Post, they say hello, and Zezenie is welcoming and relaxed and speaks dialect. Ingrid carries the small suitcase up the hill, away from the sea and the nerve-racking sounds and into the silence. Her new home has dragon's heads at the ends of the roof ridge and a weather vane and is surrounded by tall, swaying trees, their leaves rustling in the evening breeze, but this too is a form of silence.

She feels stupid as they go inside, like when she started school, but, tactfully, Zezenie doesn't notice, and shows Ingrid where she will stay, as if she has created the room with her own hands. Ingrid admires the drawers and cupboards and doesn't see the lady of the house walking closely past her, sniffing, to check whether she smells, but she does see when Zezenie takes her hands to welcome her for a second time, and examines her nails. However, Ingrid has scrubbed them under the watchful eye of Maria, so she stands there calmly as the inspection takes place, and as they go downstairs, for further instruction in the kitchen, she considers she has passed the test, and will also be able to surmount the challenges ahead: a stove with blue tiles from Delft in Holland is, after all, lit in the same way as a black cast-iron stove on Barrøy, it just doesn't heat as well, though it stays in for a longer time, and coke is no more difficult than peat, it is easier.

Here we have the living rooms, Zezenie says, three rooms which form a kind of step up to the most private area of the house, where there is a stove too, but Ingrid has to light the fire here only once a day, at five o'clock in the afternoon, so that it is warm at seven o'clock, when the man of the house comes home from work, and there is the clock she should go by, an heirloom with pendulums and Roman numerals and brass bobs, which she has to wind up once every fourth day. Otherwise she has no business in here, and the children are not allowed to play here, either.

Ingrid wonders why she was ever fearful, perhaps she just waited on the island too long, she thinks, it wasn't that the world didn't want her, she may have misread the situation, and she is not going to make the same mistake again; the possibility that it might have been her mother who held her back, Maria's loneliness, doesn't cross her mind.

40

After the happy period preparing for confirmation at the rectory, the transition to life at the house of Oskar Tommesen and his wife was not so wonderful. And it was certainly complicated. In the first place, the children were not like the priest's. The older one was seven, and for some reason didn't go to school. His name was Felix and he screeched like an animal when he didn't get what he wanted, then his mother went out of the room and left it to Ingrid to calm him down.

The other child was a girl of three, Suzanne. Most of the time she lay in a cradle big enough for a man, or sat on her mother's or Ingrid's lap and didn't seem interested in anything. At other times she was pushed around by Ingrid, outdoors as well in a small wooden pram decorated with flower patterns, when Zezenie sent her to do the shopping or down to the Trading Post to get some fish.

Ingrid enjoyed these walks to the Store, which was a daily occurrence, wheeling a pram with a small child made her feel five years older, a person with responsibility. She took pride in her appearance and the clothes she wore, and talked to people as soon as they talked to her, and smiled, so they carried on talking to her, Ingrid was a good-natured, friendly young person from the islands, strange as it may seem.

But then there was this feeble child, who wasn't toilet-trained yet, and couldn't even sit upright on the floor, let alone walk. Ingrid thought there might be something wrong with her. Zezenie would hear none of it, Suzanne was just a bit delicate. The word had an elegant ring to it, like porcelain.

But there was something wrong with the mistress of the house too, unless she was just doing what people of her class normally did. She would be sewing and then suddenly jump up with a cry and run out of the house and down to the Trading Post, where her husband Oskar had reigned since his father became poorly, then return with either a smile on her lips or crying her eyes out, and with dishevelled hair, occasionally in both states at the same time. Then she would question why Ingrid had given Felix something to eat, which she'd had to do, partly to quieten him down, but mainly because the clock had struck.

His mother patted him cautiously on the head, as if afraid of burning her fingers, then went up to the first floor to rest, but only after opening the window to give the room an airing, a procedure Ingrid had never heard of, fancy airing a room there weren't any fumes in, and she didn't reappear until after darkness had fallen, when Ingrid had long since given the children their supper and the man of the house came in and sat down in the most private of the living rooms to smoke his pipe.

From the kitchen Ingrid could hear husband and wife

laughing and arguing and shouting at each other and then laughing again, switching from one to the other so quickly that after a week or so she began to go to bed early; the same exhausting form of coexistence was played out across the dining table, she didn't feel able to provide satisfactory answers to their questions or follow what they were laughing at.

The Trading Post owner's son was polite and distant, vague and jovial. He collected stamps in a big ledger and copperplates of Napoleon and Danish and Swedish kings who had reigned in Norway, which he spread out over the large living-room table and which it was Ingrid's job to tidy up in the correct order. He also had a particular way of eyeing her, and winking, when Zezenie wasn't looking. And he didn't know how to separate fish from the bone, he just placed a large piece of cod on his plate, plunged his fork into it and lifted the fish with the skin and bones into his mouth, only to pick out with his fingers all the bits that didn't belong in his stomach, which was very difficult when he was talking at the same time.

In addition, he wore spectacles, which were always fogged up. Ingrid asked whether she should clean them. Then he sent her such a nebulous look that she didn't catch what he said. She thought there must be something bothering him, he was fragile, just like his son, whom he never talked to, it was a house where the parents and children lived in separate worlds.

All this amounted to one small disappointment after another in a wealthy household where there was absolutely no need for anything at all not to live up to Ingrid's expectations.

There wasn't much to do, they didn't even have any animals, and every week an elderly woman from a small farmstead in the gorge behind the church came to scrub all the nine rooms with green soap – except for Ingrid's, she had to do that herself – and the kitchen too. She arrived in darkness and left in darkness, and was often not paid, Ingrid noticed. Zezenie stood there without so much as a hint of embarrassment on her face and declared that she didn't have any money today, Ingeborg could buy things on credit for the time being, couldn't she?

The old lady never said a word, she was silent and crooked and surrounded by a strange smell – lard? But she shooed away the children as if they were in the way, and they weren't, Ingrid saw to that, Ingrid saw to most things, she had made the house her own, including its strange customs, she had begun to defend it, to herself too, soon she might even be able to regard the master of the house's fish-eating habits as normal.

But she hadn't been there for more than three months when a message came from the Trading Post to the effect that Oskar Tommesen had taken the steamer to the town, as planned, but hadn't returned.

There might of course have been many reasons for this, but none of them plausible, and Zezenie spent the rest of the evening walking around the house wringing her hands, unable to answer the questions Ingrid had inferred it could be of advantage to ask from time to time, for a maidservant.

When the husband didn't show up the following day either, nor the next, the mother quite simply lost all interest in the children and wandered around like a bedraggled ghost taking stock of the fixtures and furnishings and noting everything down in a book with a hard cover, then sorting and packing it all in large suitcases. She was surrounded by light and sound, at night too, three days and two nights. Then she too disappeared, without a word, she simply wasn't there when Ingrid got up one morning and went down to get the stove going and make coffee, the house was as quiet as the grave and dark, quieter than it had ever been before.

She waited until the clock chimed, got the children out of bed, fed them and started waiting. Nothing happened. She went up and knocked at the parents' bedroom door, no answer, she peeped in, the double bed was made, no-one there. Ingeborg arrived to scrub the floors, obviously understood what had happened and mumbled, well, that was the way of the world, this bankruptcy that everyone had been expecting, maybe it wasn't written in the stars, but it was certainly written between the lines in the newspaper.

Ingrid had no idea what a bankruptcy was. She didn't read the newspaper either, it came out three times a week, and when the old woman muttered something about the Tommesens probably having gone to America, her head began to spin.

Ingeborg hadn't even removed her coat, she sat in the large, empty kitchen drinking coffee for the first time, from a cup with a gold rim, telling Ingrid that things had gone from bad to worse with the business ever since the old man fell ill.

Ingrid felt confused relief that at least this didn't have anything to do with her. But it certainly did, she had been left sitting in charge of two children who were not hers. And there would be no floor-washing today, Ingeborg drank up her coffee and said she definitely wouldn't be coming back.

"But hva am A goen' t' do?" Ingrid exclaimed.

"Well, hva ar we goen' t' do?" the old woman said, and left.

Ingrid regretted not crying a long time ago. Now, when no-one could see, it was too late.

41

From her window Ingrid had a view of the sea and the islands. Barrøy was darker than the others, perhaps because it had more grass than cliffs and rocks. She saw the island every evening, said goodnight, and saw it again in the morning, sometimes clearly, at other times like a hovering shadow, now it was autumn and dark and there was nothing to see.

She got up and made some food, extinguished the lamps and played with the children, lit the lamps, played with the children, it was Felix's turn for a bath, supper, Suzanne to bed, followed by Felix, who didn't ask for his mother a single time, but walked around the house hitting the furniture with a stick, Ingrid took it off him, which occasioned more screams.

The next night she didn't sleep at all. But yet again she got up at six, prepared breakfast for three and ate alone, waited beside two unused plates until the clocks struck before going up to wake the children, fed and dressed them and set off on a walk with them, it was raining and of course she ought to knock on a door somewhere and ask what she should do.

But where?

She went to the rectory, but it was all dark there. She walked back home and played and ate and washed up, lit the lamps and wound up the clocks, no one had a bath today, thank God.

This time she slept like a log.

But was woken by the silence. And her crying. She opened the window, listened to the sea and went back to sleep, got up and went downstairs and set the table for three adults and two children, she was one of the adults, waited for light to stream through the windows, woke the children and made Felix dress himself, slapped him when he howled. She went downstairs with Suzanne, and Felix followed, semi-dressed and whining. She helped him to put on the rest of his clothes and said that a seven-year-old not being able to dress himself was a disgrace. He ran outside in his stockinged feet, she ran after him and dragged him back in and forced him to sit at the table. After the meal she helped him to put on his outdoor clothes, dressed Suzanne and walked down to the wharf with both children where she waited for the steamer.

The steamer arrived in light snow, unloaded goods, took on board milk and fish and was gone.

What were all the glares supposed to mean?

There was another walk around the village, in the hope that someone should catch sight of them. But no one stopped and no one asked and thought it was nice of her to take on the burden of two rich man's children. She arrived back home and lit the lamps and cooked and bathed Suzanne and sat talking to deaf ears until she fell asleep, not even Suzanne mentioned her mother.

Next day the steamer came.

And left.

Ingrid walked around with the children. Without attracting any attention. Margot at the Store said of course the parents would be coming back, but added that Ingrid perhaps shouldn't take all the items she had placed on the counter, who was going to pay for them . . . ?

Ingrid looked at her with a vacant expression.

There was talk of new owners taking over the Trading Post, but . . .

Another sleepless night. And the next morning brought neither new nor old owners. Ingrid packed her little case and again stood on the wharf with two children watching the steamer dock and depart.

But there was also the milk-run boat, loading empty milk churns, the converted fishing smack belonging to her father's childhood friend, Paulus.

Ingrid walked down the gangway with Suzanne in her arms and holding Felix's hand and said she wanted to go with him. From the window of his wheelhouse, Paulus said that was out of the question. Ingrid went back ashore and collected the suitcase and the little pram, put Suzanne in it, covered her with blankets and sat down on the ground holding the pram between her knees. Felix sat down beside her. Paulus came down to the deck and repeated that he couldn't take them, if he did he would need the parents' permission, on top of that the weather was bad, he wasn't even sure he could make it to Barrøy. Ingrid didn't answer. She cried and sat motionless. Felix was silent.

42

They were received by Barbro and Maria, who were stand-ing on Barrøy's quay in the gale with two milk churns, staring down at the deck, in absolute amazement, where Ingrid had gone to sleep and was now waking up, stiff and sore. The children were seasick and had thrown up. They managed to get them ashore, Paulus, cursing, lifted them up one after the other, also the pram, for which there was no use on the island. But at least they could carry it between them, like a stretcher, with Suzanne in it.

Felix perked up and walked without assistance. And now he was holding Ingrid's hand.

Ingrid had to repeat her story four or five times once they were in the warm, until she fell asleep on the kitchen bench, she babbled on and was full to the brim with feelings no-one can articulate, the relief at being home again isolated in the sea with two children who weren't hers and whom she couldn't stand.

Two days later Maria went to the mainland in an attempt to find a solution to the mystery, but returned none the wiser, the children's grandfather was muddled, the priest's wife still wasn't back, and Margot at the store . . .?

Another week passed.

With bad weather and two days without the milk run. Maria went over again, with the same meagre outcome.

Meanwhile Suzanne slept with Ingrid while Felix was on his own in the double bed in the North Chamber. He had stopped screaming after trying it once and being stopped by Barbro, who forced him to go with her to the cowshed and wanted to teach him how to milk, her son could, even though he wasn't a woman. Felix cried and milked the cows without ever saying he missed anyone. He wanted toys and was given tools to play with. That stopped him crying. They gave him clothes that Lars had grown out of. And after three days he was on the sea with Ingrid holding a jig, although he could neither row nor bleed a fish, a boy who had grown up in a family dealing in fish and he couldn't do this.

But Ingrid was patient and back home in her own waters. Felix listened and fumbled and was there again the day after. He fetched wood and peat when they asked him to and could turn the handle of the cream separator, with Barbro, and in the house Suzanne crawled around on the kitchen floor babbling and ready to walk at any moment.

She had her potty training on Lars's chair. Maria sat holding her between her knees and let go. She fell. Barbro did the same. Suzanne fell and crawled and fell, and later the same evening Felix climbed up into Barbro's lap and was impossible to budge. She sat with him until he fell asleep. Then they carried him up to bed. And Ingrid sensed this power that only a bird can feel as it sits on the ridge of a hill, wings outstretched, letting the wind do the rest.

When the children had been there for ten days Lars returned from school on Havstein. Rowing. He had been fishing on the way, moored the boat to the ladder beneath the crane on the quay, looked up and caught sight of an unfamiliar face.

"Hvo's tha?"

"A'm Felix," Felix said.

Lars clambered up, hauled a fish onto the quay and cleaned it on the workbench while Felix stood watching. He split the fish and salted most of it in a tub and cut up the rest to eat fresh, put the bits in a pail and carried it home together with his satchel. Felix followed him. When they went in Lars asked once more who the boy was. His mother gave him the same answer. Felix. So did Ingrid, who was sitting by the window knitting. On the floor sat a little girl chewing the wooden handle of a gaff.

"And hvo's tha?" Lars said.

"Suzanne," Ingrid replied.

Lars put down the pail of fish on the bench beside the water buckets, where he knew his mother wouldn't want it. She told him off. Lars grinned. She asked if it had been plain rowing. He said yes.

"Well, the weither's fair nu," Barbro said, starting to rinse the fish again, which wasn't necessary as Lars had done it. He stood watching her with the same grin.

"Hva's tha grinnen' a'?" Barbro said.

"A' tha," he said, going into the hall and taking off his coat and boots. When he came back in, Felix was standing in the middle of the floor looking at him. Lars sat down at the table. Felix went up to him.

"Tha'll have t' get th' taters nu," Barbro said.

Felix gave a start and went out, returned with a bucket and gave it to Barbro. She looked into it and appeared to be considering whether to say something.

"Hva's wrong, Mamma?" Lars said. "Aren't thar enough taters?"

"Ya."

"So hva's wrong?"

"It's nothin'. Hva's tha babblen' about?"

"A see hva A ca' see."

"An' hva ca' tha see?"

Lars didn't answer. He glanced over at Ingrid waiting for her to ask if he had seen Nelly on Havstein. Lars had a think and then said yes. Ingrid knitted and asked hvur Nelly war doen'? Lars shrugged and looked at her knitting, asked her what it was going to be. She held it up and showed him the sleeve of a jumper. He reached a hand across the table and felt the knitting between his fingers.

"Hvo's it f'r?"

"F'r me."

Ingrid put her arm in the sleeve and showed him, clenched her fist and spread her fingers like petals, the way Zezenie did when she tried on dresses, there was ribbing round the wrist and a star pattern around the top of the sleeve, the wool was blue and the stars white, she had dyed the yarn herself. Lars nodded. Ingrid knitted. Maria came in from the barn and spotted Lars, she put down a bucket of cream and went to the pantry for a sieve, looked at Lars again and said:

"Tha'll have t' row th' boat in. Th' weither is goen' t' bluster."

"After somethin' t' eat," Lars said.

"Nu!" Maria said, and went back out.

Lars eyed Felix, who was still standing there, staring at him.

"Tha comen'?"

"Ya," Felix said.

43

The day before Lars was due to start school again, the milk-run boat was unable to put in at Barrøy, but it could two days later. Lars was still there, weather-bound.

And Hans Barrøy stepped ashore on his own island, having come home from his labouring job a month early. He had a black pipe coiled around his upper body, like a bandolier, a wooden crate was hoisted onto land together with his kitbag. No-one knew why he had returned now.

But they were happy.

Her relief at a husband coming home alive, even though his return is so unexpected. The country and the world is in crisis, bankruptcies and tight budgets, people are forced to leave their farms, others lose their jobs, and the blasting crew he had been the foreman of has been laid off with no more pay than he has already spent, on this:

The pipe was a hose meant for oil, but it was new and clean and could be used for water just as well as oil, and here is a pump and a filter and connectors. He had them in the crate, together with dies for cutting threads on copper piping, so that they could finally have water in the kitchen, this should have been done ages ago, so now was the time, before the frost got into the ground.

"Hvo's tha?" he said to Felix who came and took Barbro's hand, looking more like Lars than any of the others had noticed, a copy of Lars, and what was more he was wearing Lars's clothes.

At his side stood the real Lars, a man of twelve years, who looked up at his mother and asked if he could stay, he didn't want to go back to Havstein. He shot a glance at Paulus, who was standing on the deck with his hands on his hips, hva's it goen' t' be then? He wanted his hawsers back.

Before Barbro could answer Lars dropped his bag on the quay and set off at a run in a southerly direction. They stood there watching him. Hans laughed and said to Paulus:

"Tha'd bitter go then."

He let go of the ropes. Paulus pulled them in, shook his head and disappeared into the wheelhouse. Then they walked home with the crate and kitbag and an oil hose and two empty milk churns, it was a veritable clock, this connection they now had with the rest of the world, a clockwork mechanism, if not particularly well oiled.

Next morning Hans sent the children off around the island to collect moss in peat baskets. He knocked a hole in the foundation wall under the pantry, and for the next few days he and Lars lay on their backs beneath the floor constructing a narrow, ten-metre-long wooden box below the joists. Felix and Ingrid stood outside and passed in materials whenever they shouted for them, since the rainwater tank was at the southern end of the house and the kitchen in the north. Then they knocked a hole in the tank wall and fitted the filter a metre below the water level, threaded the hose through the box, drilled a hole in the floor and pushed it up into the kitchen, it was only half a metre too long. There they installed the pump above the sink and connected the pipes.

But the moss wasn't dry yet. It had been spread out across the floor of the barn loft and was to be used as insulation around the piping in the box. And there was still no frost.

The question was whether this job was urgent.

It was. Hans dried the moss in the kitchen, in eight fish crates which he hung from the ceiling above the stove. The house smelled of summer, haymaking, especially up in the room Felix and Lars now shared, the North Chamber, it too had a hatch in the floor.

Hans rowed over to the Trading Post in the *færing* and tried to talk to the old owner. He found him in the house of an elderly married couple where he was being taken care of for money they no longer received and muttered that a tragedy had befallen his son. He had heard about the children, yes, he wept and said:

"They should bide hvar they ar'."

"Hvar?" said Hans. "On Barrøy?"

The old man stared at the wall.

Hans had known this man all his life, he was a prince and a chieftain on this coast, and he had cursed him countless times, a man who lived off others' labour, but the sight of him lying here as the wretched result of his own privileged life gave him no satisfaction.

Hans left and went to see the priest, who was back again after an autumn in the neighbouring parish.

Johannes Malmberget had also heard about the children and Ingrid's plight, but excused the local community, saying they were afflicted by the same view of the rich as everybody else, life is hell. There was also good reason to believe that young Tommesen had taken his own life, Malmberget added in hushed tones. And his wife was at an asylum in Bodø, there had to be limits to people gloating over others' misfortune, he was going to mention this in his sermon on Sunday, which he was working on at this very moment, would Hans care for a dram?

Yes, please, he wouldn't say no.

He had three. And they got no further than that they would have to wait and see, maybe Zezenie had family and they would make their presence known, though the priest rather doubted it, Hans was unable to work out why. Then, out of the blue, Hans said:

"Can't tha teik 'em in?"

"Hvo?"

"Th' kids."

"Me?"

"Yes, tha."

Johannes Malmberget looked down at his lap, his eyes wandered along the walls before returning to Hans Barrøy, then he lowered them apologetically and mumbled that the local welfare system wasn't up to much, it was no more than poor relief, and these children were rich, or had been, this was what their two gazes were fighting a silent duel about, what to do with the rich when they are reduced to poverty, logic inverted, history in reverse, it is as nonsensical as claiming that water flows upwards.

Karen Louise came and stood in the doorway, looking as though she was planning to offer them some refreshment, but then she was gone again, and they sat for a while longer until Hans Barrøy got to his feet and thanked the priest for the dram and shook him by the hand.

The priest returned the thanks.

Hans Barrøy went to the Store and did some shopping, more than he could afford, as usual, but he could still rely on his good name, and sailed out of the fjord in a rosy evening light which augured a change of weather, an easterly wind and frost. He thought about the moss in the crates in the kitchen and mumbling as he did so:

"Matutinum, matutinum . . ."

This is Latin and means tomorrow, tomorrow, he had seen it in a prayer book at the railway site, and the words had stayed with him, like pearls in his mouth. It was rare for him to be struck by a sense of solemnity at being home again on his own island, this man who knew all there was to know about longing for home without going to pieces, now at last it was proved beyond all doubt, at the priest's too, that when everything else fails, the island is a rock, he already knew that of course, but had never felt it so religiously as now when the world was askew and he had a greater burden on his shoulders than ever before, he thought as he dropped sail off the coast so the *færing* could glide the last few yards until iron bit into wood.

But he didn't go up to the house.

He lifted out his purchases, winched the boat into the shed, sat on the step, got out his pipe and noticed that he wasn't able to straighten the fingers of his right hand, as if he were still holding the tiller. He smoked and looked north at the rosy sunlight, which slowly turned blue. And that was where they found him, dead.

By that time he was so stiff that it looked as though he was sitting even when they laid him down. They were unable to straighten him out, and they couldn't look at him, so they threw a blanket over him, and the one person who had the strength to launch the *færing* again and sail back to the Trading Post to bear the news was Lars.

44

It was the most pointless of deaths on a very long coast. Hans Martinsen Barrøy was no more than fifty, and as strong as a bear. Pastor Malmberget came to the island with his mouth full of words such as stricken and suffering, and also some maritime terms, he never forgot the context of his duties, and he was just as petrified of the sea as he had always been. Is there anything more terrifying than waves, he thought, as he arrived, exhausted, in a heavy shower of rain and with his eyes swimming only to find that Maria had placed her hands in her lap and been struck dumb. As had her daughter Ingrid.

And what was it about that look in Lars's eyes?

Barbro stood with her back turned, scolding the little girl, and avoided looking at the priest, their whole existence had been turned upside down, and Johannes Malmberget had to make all the arrangements himself, having the body shipped to the main island and organising the funeral.

When the day arrived, Adolf from Malvika and Thomas from Stangholmen took it upon themselves to bring the family over on yet another day of stormy weather to the most basic of funeral services the priest had ever officiated at, whereafter he pressed his hands together and mumbled his rituals. He would come over to the island and see how they were doing at regular intervals, and also attend to the matter of the children. Maria replied with the only words she uttered in the course of those days, was he thinking of taking the children away from them, too?

The day after the funeral Lars got up and lit the stove, cut down the fish crates which were hanging over it, woke Ingrid and told her to brew some coffee for Maria and Barbro. Ingrid didn't want to get up.

Lars said she had no choice.

There was something about that look in his eyes.

For the rest of the day he and Felix lay on their backs beneath the floor stuffing moss into the piping box and nailing it up again. Then they bricked up the hole in the foundation wall. Lars was finished with school, that much was plain for anybody with eyes in their heads to see. He took the boat and rowed over to Moltholmen with some tools and hammered an anchor bolt into the rock face. Felix was with him and had to hold a rag around the chisel so that chips wouldn't fly out when he hit it with the hammer, he asked what Lars was making.

Lars told him to wait and see.

They rowed back to Barrøy and went into the quay house and fetched five nets, rowed out to Moltholmen again with a pulley block and an anchor rope, fixed the pulley, threaded the rope round it and rowed back to Barrøy with it, where they also hammered in an iron bolt. Then they drew out a string of five nets, closing off half the sound, and pulled it a little further so it was suspended midway.

Barbro had been watching them from the house and came to ask them what they were doing. Lars said that now they could fish from the land. Even in bad weather, cod and pollack swam through the sound, and flounder, in the summer they could catch salmon too. He was also going to put nets across the sound between Barrøy and Gjesøya, and Barrøy and the nearer of the two Skarvholmen islets, that would make fifteen nets in all.

Barbro shook her head.

Lars said it was something Hans had talked about doing when he was too old to go out in a boat. Barbro went back to the house and told Maria what they were doing. Maria didn't react, she and Ingrid sat with their knitting in their laps, looking as if they were imitating each other. Barbro started cooking. Now Suzanne was big enough to stand beside the table and sink her teeth into the edge. No-one laughed at her. She fell and got up again and held on with her teeth and stayed there. Ingrid wept and knitted until Lars came in and told her to go with him to Gjesøya, the sound was too wide, the weather too bad and Felix too small.

Felix came in and screamed that he wasn't too small.

All three of them went, hammered an iron peg into the northern tip of Gjesøya and one on each of the two Skarvholmen islets and set three nets across the last sound. By that time it was evening. They went into the quay house and cut up a few salted fish and got some potatoes from the cellar and went back to the house. About time too, Barbro said.

"Bitty Suzanne ca' stand nu," she said, washing the potatoes as the others sat watching Suzanne. Lars glanced at Maria, who looked as if she was sleeping with her eyes open. He commented that this was the first time they had enough chairs on Barrøy.

"No, it's not," Maria said.

That was all she said that day.

The following day she said nothing.

Lars, Ingrid and Felix pulled in the nets and filled three crates with cod and pollack and gutted the fish in the quay house, tied the tails of the cod together in pairs, carried them over to the drying rack and hung them up, filleted the pollack and took them home, they were big ones. Barbro minced them for fishcakes, and fried them, and boiled potatoes and carrots, and Suzanne could walk three steps before falling. And so the days passed. Without Maria saying a word. Ingrid slept with her in the South Chamber, Felix and Lars in the North Chamber, Suzanne with Barbro. Ingrid's room was empty. No-one slept there.

When ten days had passed, Lars asked Maria whether they had any money, they needed to buy some provisions. Maria didn't answer. Ingrid heard what he said and took him up to the South Chamber, showed him what they had in the small drawer in her mother's chest, told him they were due some money from the dairy before Christmas, but it wasn't much.

He replied she would have to go to the Store with him before Christmas and repeated he didn't want Felix going.

"Hvafor?"

"Th' sea meiks 'im sick."

"An' tha an' all."

Lars countered that he was used to it and Felix wouldn't sit still in the boat and had sores on his hands that wouldn't heal because of the salt and the frost. Ingrid said she would have a look. They went down to the kitchen and asked Maria what they needed from the Store. She didn't answer. She had also begun to smell. Ingrid decided to force her to wash, knowing that she would fail. She asked Barbro what they needed. Barbro reeled off a number of items, carrots, sugar . . . Lars wrote them down on an old Thursday he tore out of the calendar and stuffed it in his pocket. Then they heard the boat horn, and went out to meet the milk run.

They exchanged milk churns. But on the deck was a trunk which Ingrid immediately recognised as Paulus wrapped straps around it to hoist it ashore, it was Zezenie's. She pulled Paulus aside, and said:

"Mamma's teiken sick."

"Hva's wrong w' her?"

"A think she's suff'ren' fro' bad nerves."

Paulus fastened the other rope, and helped them to carry the trunk up to the house, they put it on the bench in the kitchen and he began to chat to Maria, who still didn't answer, she didn't realise that he was in the room. He stood there looking around. Lars and Felix were staring at him with bloodshot eyes and salt-streaked faces, long, wet, straggly hair. Paulus asked them if they were getting any sleep. Lars said yes, a bit. Suzanne stood unsteadily next to the stove with one hand holding Barbro's skirt and the other in her mouth. Barbro had her back turned to him, she didn't seem to be aware that he was here either, this milk-run skipper, he was never here. Then she shouted at the wall that they weren't getting any sleep, they were out fishing all the time, it was terrible, they were going to pieces.

Paulus said that Ingrid should go back to the boat with him, he had something for her. She accompanied him and was told that it was serious with Maria, he was going to report it, and someone would come to help them.

He went on board and came back with a letter, scrutinised her face and asked whether she was getting any sleep. Ingrid looked at the letter, then up at him. He shook his head and untied the mooring ropes and said she should keep the boys away from the sea, under the present circumstances, Barbro was right, he said.

Ingrid said yes.

He went back on board and reversed into the gale.

In the kitchen at home they had opened Zezenie's trunk. It contained a dinner service, on which the words KÖNIGZELT, MADE IN POLAND were written, it was stacked between pages of the newspaper Ingrid didn't read when she was a maidservant at the Tommesens'.

They picked out one item at a time, piled them up on the kitchen table and saved the paper. There were twelve large dinner plates with a gold rim and a flower pattern, twelve large dishes, twelve smaller ones, twelve saucers and twelve bowls. There was twelve of everything except cups, of which there were only eleven, and one of those had no handle. Then there were two gravy boats and two dishes with lids to serve potatoes in and four large serving plates, two round and two oval, two cream jugs of different sizes, a sugar bowl with a lid, a coffee jug with a lid and a thick round bowl, God knows what that was for, but it was just as fancy as all the rest. Barbro said they could use it for gruel, a sort of halfway house between the cooking pot and the dishes. At the bottom of the trunk was a green velvet bag with a gold string and twenty-four tiny silver spoons, they were black. Barbro made room for them in the pantry. Lars and Felix carried the trunk up to the North Chamber. Ingrid boiled some halibut, with a few drops of vinegar in the water and two bay leaves, she had learned that from Zezenie. They ate off the new plates and had clotted sour cream to finish off. Suzanne broke one of the plates. Barbro went into the pantry and fetched another, and said that if Suzanne broke that one too she would get a slap. After the meal Ingrid tended to Felix's sores and told him to keep them dry for a few days. Felix sent Lars a quizzical look.

45

They couldn't go out in the boat for three days, but fished with nets from the shore and tied most of the cod in pairs by the tail and hung them up to dry, salted the rest, milked and fed the animals and let the sheep out until they gave up in the bad weather and huddled together in front of the barn door, they wanted to go out when they were in, and to go in when they were out.

And there was no trip to the Store.

Ingrid didn't manage to wash Maria, either. But after the storms subsided and they had got ready to sail to the mainland, Pastor Malmberget arrived on the milk run boat, accompanied by a doctor. He examined Maria and decided they would have to take her back with them. Ingrid packed the little suitcase that she and Barbro had used when they thought they were leaving the island.

Once the three of them had left she told Lars the trip to the mainland would have to wait. Lars asked why, they were short of almost everything. Ingrid didn't answer. So Lars didn't say any more, either.

Ingrid removed the bedding in the South Chamber and

washed it in the boiler they had in the Swedes' boathouse and hung it up to dry in the quay house. She made the bed with fresh linen and said that Barbro wouldn't need to complain anymore about not having enough space in her own bed, from now on Suzanne would be sleeping with her. Barbro said there was no need. Ingrid said she would be the judge of that. Barbro smiled and kept quiet. Suzanne's bedclothes were moved to the South Chamber and Ingrid started to teach her to walk, systematically and mercilessly, dressed her and took her out. When it was pouring down they walked back and forth in the quay house or in the boat shed, or in the sitting room.

Lars and Felix went fishing, in a boat using the gill nets from land. Felix's sores healed and opened up again, they were like swollen white mouths with tiny blood-red tongues. But he didn't fall so much anymore and sustained no new sores. Ingrid and Barbro milked and fed the animals and cooked. Suzanne was walking better with every day that passed and had also started speaking.

"Stove hot."

"Yes."

"An' th' chimeney."

Two days before Christmas the wind dropped enough for them to row over to buy some things, they didn't dare raise the sail, and Felix was sick the whole way across, throwing up and wanting to die, but recovered as soon as he had terra firma under his feet. He hadn't seen his home for two months. But there was the house, large and in darkness, with a creaking weather vane behind tall, leafless trees, he didn't even seem to recognise it. But then he said:

"Thar's heim."

"No, it isn't," Ingrid said.

They went to the Store and bought a sack of carrots, Lars swore that this was the last time they were going to waste money on them, they were going to grow carrots themselves on Barrøy. And they bought paraffin and flour and the other items he had written down on the Thursday in November he had torn out of the calendar, without answering Margot's questions, she had become friendly again, but Ingrid gave her the cold shoulder and Lars called her a bastard when they came out again.

Felix laughed, impressed. This time he didn't even notice his childhood home. But Ingrid noticed something: there was no longer anything strange about the look in Lars's eyes.

They didn't hoist the sail on the way back either, they rowed, and there were Barbro and Suzanne waiting on the shore, both crying. Lars asked them what the matter was. Barbro didn't answer, just swung the sack of carrots onto her back and walked off. Ingrid told Suzanne she wasn't going to carry her anymore, no, never. She had to make her own way up, even if she had to crawl.

She did crawl too, the last fifty metres, but she was upright on the first two slopes.

The next day the sea was calm. The sky was bluish-black and as lustrous as a luminescent sea. The family rowed out to

Skogsholmen to select the best juniper to use as a Christmas tree, as always on the day before Christmas Eve. Ingrid had read the handwritten letter that came with Zezenie's things. It contained a secret Ingrid would never share with the others because it said in handwritten ink that Zezenie was in hospital in Bodø, but would soon be back despite both the Trading Post and the house having been sold at auction, though they were not yet occupied.

Ingrid didn't know how to react.

On the trip over to Skogsholmen she said that when they returned home with the Christmas tree, Lars and Felix should have a bath, in the tub, in the barn, it couldn't be helped that it was frosty. In addition, they should all get her father's fishing gear ready for when Uncle Erling came over, so that he could take it to Lofoten, they would get at least half a catch share for it, and that was several hundred kroner. Ingrid knew how to set up a long line with hooks. So did Lars. And Felix could learn.

46

But they weren't quick enough. The *Barrøyværing* moored at the quay on December 26, a few days earlier than usual, with one irate Uncle Erling at the wheel, the bloody priest hadn't informed him about his brother's decease until the 23rd, by telegram, which had to be carried by boat via far too many islands, now they hadn't even had time to prepare for the new season. His wife Helga was also on board, and their eighteen-year-old son, Arnold, as well as three other fishermen.

But where is Maria?

My oh my, everythin's goen' t' pot hier.

They had brought half a pig with them and a bucket of sausages. Helga and Barbro and Ingrid scrubbed the whole house and lit the fires in all the rooms, even in old Martin's little room, where Helga installed herself with suitcase, Bible, embroidered tablecloth and a Christmas altar, while the crew slept on board.

Lars wanted to go with him to Lofoten, but that was out of the question, they were working a long way out in deep water, and he was only twelve. Lars argued that he could stay on land, work in the shed and bait the hooks.

"We got baiters enough," Erling said, and ordered him to stay on Barrøy and look after the family. And, what was more, continue going to school. Helga would stay until Maria came back.

"She's comen' heim, A s'pose?"

They didn't know.

The crew and Lars and Ingrid and Felix stood in the quay house setting up lines all Christmas, tied rope to the sinkers and prepared the floats and anchor ropes and tubs, managed to finish two sets in Hans's distinctive style thereby qualifying for a full catch share in Uncle Erling's generous profit-sharing scheme. They were ready on January 3 and headed north in another gale while Ingrid and Lars and Felix were left on the quay with their own plans.

This was because it wasn't such plain sailing with Helga.

She was disappointed that Maria wasn't there and made no bones about it. She was also annoyed that none of them would talk about their parents and they would turn their backs on her when she tried to find out what had happened. Not only that, she was God-fearing and a stickler for cleanliness and took over her sister-in-law's role, as though Barbro didn't know how to manage a house. And she wouldn't let Felix go out fishing, a seven-year-old in an open boat in winter, that's unheard of.

Barbro told their guest to be careful not to burn up the little peat they had in Martin's old room. Helga knew nothing about the snowed-up stacks of peat and began to get cold at night and had to be given an extra eiderdown. Furthermore, she preferred not to go to the cowshed as she was the wife of a skipper and had her own maid at home on Buøy. Not even Suzanne would have anything to do with her, Ingrid made sure of that, and Felix didn't say a word when she asked him to do something, instead he stood beside Barbro waiting until Helga occupied herself with something else. Then he did it.

Plans for Lars to start school again came to nothing, he simply stayed at home, walked around wearing the expression of a man for whom the new housekeeper was non-existent. Felix went fishing with him for as long as he had the strength, otherwise it was Ingrid. They hung up the cod and ate the pollack they didn't salt, the haddock, too, which Helga made fishcakes from, they ate them off Polish porcelain, and they were no more than a couple of weeks into the New Year when, one evening when she was sitting in old Martin's rocking chair watching Suzanne running to and fro across the floor, she said, well, it was time to go back home, there was nothing more to be done here.

Two days later she left with Paulus on the milk-run boat, together with her Bible and the altar and the whole kit and caboodle. Ingrid was the only person to give her a hug. But Barbro put on a friendly smile, as she stood with Suzanne's hand in hers explaining to the tiny tot how to wave to a boat leaving an island.

"Nu tha can wave t'em."

On the next visit Paulus moored again with both hawsers and clambered onto the quay, he wanted to have a few words with

Lars, in future could they supply him with a few boxes of cod when he put in, there wasn't a lot of milk now, they would get almost the same price per kilo as they paid at the Trading Post, which now had a new owner, one Bang Johansen, they had started buying fish again.

"An' hvafor no' th' same?" Lars said.

"Transportation," Paulus said.

"Tha doesn't have t' pay f' that."

"Pay f' hvad?"

"Th' oil."

Paulus smirked and said they could sort out the price when the time came. Lars said he wanted a receipt every time Paulus got fish, with the number of kilos per box, they had a steelyard on the island, so the weight would be right, and they wanted immediate payment.

Paulus laughed a lot at that and said he had never heard the like, he wanted to talk to Ingrid. Lars went to fetch Ingrid, who came and said the same as Lars. They agreed terms, though Paulus didn't have to pay every time but every third, in other words once a week, and he wouldn't be burdened with any interest when the weather was so lousy he had to give them a miss. They all laughed at that. Ingrid and Lars exchanged measured looks.

In the course of the following week Paulus received 391 kilos, the week after 443, then they were right down to eighty kilos. That was because Lars and Ingrid, on a visit to the Store, had heard that Paulus wasn't selling the fish fresh at the Trading Post but hanging it on a rack he had erected on the rocks below his farm, as dried fish commands a higher price than fresh fish, even though it constitutes only a quarter of the weight. They went to inspect Paulus's drying rack and saw that it was as well situated as their own on Barrøy, on bare rock. So in the fourth week they gave him just two boxes with only eighteen kilos in each. He asked if they had been having time off in the good weather, heh heh.

Lars said they had lost a lot of their nets and got written confirmation of the thirty-six kilos, along with some caustic comments about their drying rack looking fuller and fuller. Unconcerned, Lars went home and announced that from now on they would hang all the cod themselves, the cusk as well, and sell it ready dried at the Trading Post when the buyers and graders came some time in June, that was how they used to do it, Hans and Martin.

But Paulus wasn't to be fobbed off, now he wanted the fish ready split, for salting at the Trading Post, at a price they couldn't refuse. Ingrid and Barbro stood in the quay house splitting cod, weighing it and putting it in boxes, spread snow over it when the good Lord provided, and Paulus paid promptly. Then he also wanted the cod heads and spines, dried the way they did in Lofoten. They got some bodkins and strung the heads together and bundled the spines and hung them on the rack too, it would be guano, and they would be paid for it.

Lars had begun to calculate, he had begun to take notes and plan and think in unfamiliar, new ways, and he wanted to manage the money himself. Ingrid didn't agree to this. They yelled at each other. Barbro decided she would take care of the money and give them what was left over when spring came. Felix would get his share too. Lars objected, claiming he worked harder than Felix.

"Tha doesn't," Barbro said, and asked what they were going to do with the cod heads and spines hanging on the rack.

"It's guano," Lars said.

"Hva's that?"

"A don't reit know."

"It's manure," Ingrid said. "F'r export."

Barbro asked what export was.

"They sell it abroad," Felix said.

They eyed him.

"Hvar did tha learn that?"

"At heim."

Ingrid asked him if there were any other pearls of wisdom he had learned at heim. Felix didn't answer. Lars called Ingrid an old trout, Ingrid threatened him with the splitting knife. Barbro told them to pack it in.

"Tha 'r bloody kids, all of tha."

"No, we're not," Felix said. "We're adults."

Barbro laughed and walked back to the house. Ingrid carried on splitting and Lars said she wasn't cutting cleanly enough, there was too much meat left on the bone. Ingrid asked him if he wanted some lessons. Lars hesitated and said yes. She taught him. Felix watched and asked her who had taught her.

"Pappa did."

Lars asked why Hans hadn't taught him to do it as well. Ingrid omitted to say that her father wasn't his. Lars concentrated on the fish. Felix watched Ingrid and asked:

"Is tha my sister?"

Ingrid asked why he wanted to know.

As he couldn't find a reason she replied that she and he were neither mother and son, nor brother and sister. But that wasn't what Felix wanted to hear. And while Lars was on the quay hoisting up the rest of the catch she whispered to Felix that he was Lars's brother, only Lars didn't know, let's keep it a secret between us. Felix's eyes went moist. That was too much for Ingrid, she said that she couldn't waste any more time here and went home and remembered Zezenie's letter, she did that far too often, it came to her mind several times a day, like sudden jolts to the brain, this couldn't go on, she would have to burn it.

47

February. Wet, driving snow and yellow foam swept over the island. And the sea turned white, but they had put the nets on the seaward side and had to get them in before the weather turned even worse.

"Hva does tha say?" Lars said. "Sha' we go out?"

"Yes," Felix said.

They climbed aboard the *færing* and rowed round the Skarve skerries. The conditions were atrocious, and they had just started pulling in the nets when Felix fell head first into the sea. Lars pulled him back on board with the long boat hook, but he was himself so exhausted and numb that he wasn't able to row. They drifted sideways towards the shore while he lay holding on to Felix, who couldn't speak, and hit land on Barrøy's coast in the sound between the island and Moltholmen. He got the young boy out of the boat and wanted to do two things at the same time, carry him home and save the *færing*.

He squinted into the driving snow and felt the ice. All the way in.

And how far in is that?

He hauled Felix up on his back and started walking. It was

a long way, and Felix couldn't hold on. Ingrid saw them from the house and ran down to help them the last part of the way. They manoeuvred Felix into the kitchen, where Barbro tore off his clothes and massaged and pounded him and laid him on the bench under an eiderdown and started massaging him again, while he gabbled, his teeth chattering. Lars stood at their side, his face a ghostly white, and said they had to save the *færing*. And the nets. Ingrid told him to shut up. So did Barbro, who ordered him to take off his clothes as well, at once. He repeated that the boat had to be saved, and went back out. Ingrid put on her coat and ran after him through the snowstorm down to the sound, where the *færing* was pitching in the water, a gaping hole in its side. The rudder was broken, too. But both pairs of oars were still there, as were the two empty line tubs. Lars tore off his jumper and stuffed it in the hole, they used the oars to lever the *færing* away from the shore and rowed through the sound with the sea flooding into the mid-section, coaxed it round the headland, where the Swedes' boathouse was, beached it, bailed out the water and dragged it as far onto land as they could.

Lars screamed that they had to go out and find the nets, using the other *færing*. Ingrid asked if he was out of his mind. He was rushing back and forth like a crazy man. Ingrid shouted that he wasn't normal, he couldn't go out to sea again. He gave a shiver, grinned and asked whether she thought Felix was going to die. Ingrid said no.

She got the shivers, too, and had to go to bed.

Felix lay on the bench in the kitchen, delirious. Barbro sat at his side, during the nights, too, Suzanne wanted to as well. Ingrid noticed she was missing and got up and lay in front of the stove in the kitchen and said she was well again. Barbro made her go back up to bed, and she lay awake until Barbro came in carrying the sleeping Suzanne and placed her at her side, then sat on the bed and asked Ingrid if she was afraid of the dark. Ingrid said no. Had she had seen any ghosts, Barbro asked. Ingrid said yes. Barbro said that was because of the fever. But now she wasn't feverish anymore. Barbro could tell that by her forehead. Ingrid nodded. When Suzanne woke up next morning she asked Ingrid to teach her how to knit.

"Tha's a wain," Ingrid said.

"That's hva Mamma said," Suzanne answered.

"Hvo's Mamma?" Ingrid asked. Suzanne looked at her blankly. "A thought it war me?" Ingrid said. Suzanne hesitated, and smiled. Ingrid said she could watch while she knitted, then she would get the hang of it faster when the time came. Suzanne thought that was fine. And then she could learn to count, not just on her fingers, but by keeping track of the stitches.

48

Lars didn't fall ill. After the weather had eased he went out and found that he couldn't budge the snow-covered *færing*. He fetched Barbro. They managed to turn it round and get it onto two trestles so that he could examine the hole in the hull from both sides. It was bigger than he had imagined, one of the ribs was broken too. Barbro shook her head. Lars asked whether Felix was going to die.

Barbro said no, and added that now she bet he wished he'd paid more attention to Hans when he was repairing boats.

"Hva does tha know about tha'?" Lars said.

"It teiks two," Barbro stated pointedly, and walked back towards the house, but turned and shouted to him that she could help and hold something against the board while he hammered in the nails, the rest he would have to do himself.

Lars went into the Swedes' boathouse where Hans stored his materials and found a few planks of knot-free spruce. He sawed off a suitable piece, ripped out the broken board in the side of the boat and used it as a template. Then he needed two more bits, so he had to run in and out a few times and take measurements, then saw and plane and run out and mark the position and measure up. When he had finished he couldn't bend the board into position.

Barbro came and said he should take the board home with him, wrap it in damp cloths and leave it in a tub under the stove for a day or two, to make it more pliable. Lars asked if she could do that, he didn't want to be in the kitchen listening to Felix's gurglings, he didn't even go there to eat. Barbro said he would have to do it himself, she would find some old rags for him.

Lars said in that case he wouldn't bother.

"No, no, no," Barbro said. He had to eat anyway.

He went in with her and did as she ordered and glanced at Felix, who was lying on the bench shaking and didn't notice that Lars was there. Lars went back to the boathouse and searched for material to make a new rib. He couldn't find anything. There were two windows in the building, one facing north and one facing south. He stood for a moment gazing through the former. The sea was black and smooth. Like lead. Like tar.

He stood there surveying the view until he had seen enough.

He went out and, unseen, walked behind the knoll to the boat shed and launched the other *færing*, it was older than the damaged one, it had been in there for a long time and was dry and leaky. But it was easy to row. He rowed around the northern point of the island and was heading south through the sound when he spotted his mother on the island. She was waving both arms.

He wanted to row past, but the tone of her voice drew him towards the shore. He asked her what she wanted. She said he couldn't haul in the lines on his own. He backed the oars and Barbro stepped on board, pushed him aside, took hold of the oars, rowed out past the Skarve skerries and grasped the first anchor rope. Lars pulled in the line while Barbro rested on the oars and bailed out the water. They worked in silence. They filled one and a half rib sections with fish, a lot of it old and half-eaten, but some of it usable. Then they hauled in all the tackle.

They took one oar apiece and rowed back to the quay, where they landed the fish. Lars split them and Barbro packed them in crates, fetched some snow and sprinkled it on top. After they had finished Paulus came round the headland and drew along-side the quay, took the milk on board, what little there was of it, and also the fish, which he said was O.K., although it wasn't much of a catch and the splitting was perhaps a touch amateur-ish. Lars said he wouldn't be getting any more for a few days and was about to explain why when Barbro butted in and told Paulus they had to repair the *færing*.

Paulus nodded and went back on board.

That evening Felix stopped gurgling. His eyes were red and bleary, but he smiled over the edge of the eiderdown and asked for something to eat and drink. He didn't eat much, soon fell asleep, but slept peacefully. Lars asked once again if he was going to die.

The answer was the same.

Next morning Lars was the first up, he lit the stove and noticed that Felix was breathing heavily. Felix opened his eyes and looked at him. Lars asked if he could talk. Felix nodded.

"Hvur's it goen'?"

"Not s' bad."

Felix wanted to sit up, but couldn't. Lars asked how he was now. Again Felix mumbled "Not s' bad" and remained on his back while Lars explained that he was going to row to Skogsholmen to see whether he could find some wood to make a new boat rib. Felix nodded. It should really be pine, Lars said, but juniper would do. Felix glanced over at the window where snow lay on the glazing bars and asked what the weather was like. Lars said it was good. Felix blinked. Lars went down to the boat shed and rowed off in the old *færing*. It was still leaky, so he had to take breaks and bail out, but he found the inlet on the landward side of the islet and moored the boat to the peg Hans had fixed there, climbed onto the rock armed with an axe and saw and began searching. By then day was breaking.

He searched until it was fully light.

Then it turned dark again as a snow shower passed overhead, silent and heavy. The sea still looked like tar. When it was light once more he found an old crooked juniper tree, used the axe to loosen the coarsest roots from the frozen slope, cursing as he blunted the cutting edge, chopped the roots off one by one and sawed the trunk roughly a metre above the base, it was as thick as an arm, a young man's arm.

He walked back to the boat, bailed out and rowed home. As he rounded Moltholmen he saw Barbro waiting. Lars asked what she was doing there. She asked whether he had been fishing. He said no and wanted to know how Felix was doing.

"Not s' bad," Barbro said.

They pulled the boat ashore. Lars took the piece of juniper into the Swedes' boathouse and began to whittle it into shape. "It has t' be dried first," Barbro said.

"Hva?"

She explained that he couldn't use green timber for ribs, though juniper was better than spruce if there was no other option. He asked why. Barbro explained that juniper shrinks less, and also expands less, it is resinous and tough. Lars asked what she thought he should do. She said he should probably have a go with the juniper, then walked back to the house as he hammered away at the broken half-rib, using it as a template, and worked until darkness fell.

When Lars came in to eat, Felix was sitting upright under the eiderdown on the bench, coughing. His eyes were still red, but he swallowed a few morsels and asked in an almost inaudible voice whether Lars had got hold of any suitable wood. Lars said yes and added that he was going to clinch the pieces the following day. He asked Barbro if she had put any water on the wood in the tub under the stove. She said yes. Lars went out and worked until it was time for bed. By then Felix was alone in the kitchen, asleep.

When Lars got up next day it was dark outside the window. He dressed and went downstairs and saw that Felix was still asleep; he could tell by his breathing that he was alive and not dead.

He had something to eat, went to the boathouse and got out some nails and two hammers and practised clinch-nailing on the anvil. He found some tar and hemp, heated the tar in a bucket on a primus and cut two lengths of hemp. After dinner Barbro joined him and lay on a rug beneath the boat holding a rock while Lars lay inside it and hammered the clinches home. The boat now had a light-coloured plank and an equally light-coloured half-rib, contrasting with the other timber which was black with tar. They launched the boat, jumped on board and drifted in the wind. A few drops seeped in. Barbro said they had done a good job. What about the rudder? Lars said he would fix it the next day. They rowed around the headland, pulled the *færing* ashore and wedged it in an upright position. Barbro walked home. Using a bucket, Lars collected some seawater and poured enough into the boat to cover the repair so that the boards would expand. By the time he had finished a wind had blown up. He went to the quay house where he disentangled and repaired the line they had saved. He wondered whether to wash it as well.

Wash fishing gear in mid-season?

He decided not to, and instead slung the floats with the rest of the tackle on the baiting bench. It was dark and snowing heavily as he wended his way home. In the kitchen window he spotted a face. It was Felix, who had got up and was waiting for him.

49

The sun is high in the sky and the birds have resumed their cacophonous riot of activity, the streaks of drifted snow across the island glitter, giving it the appearance of a zebra. Barbro is sitting outside on her chair again, making nets. And Suzanne doesn't stray an inch from Ingrid's side, Ingrid who has made a discovery in the first light of day, the notion that not only her father but also her mother has gone forever, this notion which is so unbearable, which strikes her like a blast of wind, then leaves her again, and her parents are still there when she thinks about something else, her eyes wandering across the island, which is as it has always been.

She made another discovery, too.

She had fallen asleep in the sun near Love Spinney, woke and found herself alone.

She got up and looked around, Suzanne was nowhere to be seen. She started searching but to no avail. She broke into a run, to the north, then south, like a horse that has bolted. She began to scream. She gasped for breath and ran and shrieked Suzanne's name until her insides were in her throat and she didn't know who she was or what she was doing. And found Suzanne in the south of the island, sitting on the beach beside the raft collecting shells, she held up a horse-mussel shell, a large one, as white as snow and bigger than two children's hands, it was perfectly round.

Ingrid discovered she had become a mother.

It was a terrible feeling.

She collected the shells in her apron and walked Suzanne home, it would soon be feeding time in the cowshed. Ingrid said she thought shells were money when she was small, on an island they are the most perfect things you can find. She had collected huge piles of them and put some on all the windowsills of the house and barn until one day her mother told her she would have to find a place to bury her treasure. She took Suzanne with her and tried to find it again. Suzanne must have turned four this winter, she reflected, and it struck her she didn't even know when the children's birthdays were. When she thought about Suzanne and birthdays and this treasure that they didn't find she forgot her other problems, and once again the island was as it should be.

Everything changes on an island when there are only children left. Plus Barbro. Barbro has never grown up completely. In a way she has, though. And is Ingrid a child? No, she has been an adult for ten years. While Lars has been grown up ever since he was born. There are three adults and two children. Now they have fifteen new lambs and have had to bury only one, it was black and the mother had no milk, the second one had to be bottle-fed. They also have three calves, Barbro delivered them. Ingrid says they will have to carry on digging the ditches on Gjesøya, resume the work Hans set in motion. But Lars remembers the silence between him and his uncle when they left the place and Lars also has his eyes firmly fixed on the sea, like Hans, Felix has too, so when are they going to start transporting rocks across the island, from the ruins in Karvika to build a mole south of the Swedes' boathouse?

Ingrid doesn't listen.

They plough up the old potato field again with Barbro as the horse, sometimes with Lars. But there won't be any carrots grown here, they don't know what to do. They wash down the fishing gear and repair the eider-duck houses. And still there is no ditch-digging done on Gjesøya, they talk about when it should be done. Ingrid and Suzanne collect eggs, test them in water and lay them in wet sand in big and small barrels. Ingrid gives Suzanne two handfuls of down and teaches her the difference between what is merely wonderful and what is a God-given miracle. While Lars and Felix cut peat until they drop dead with exhaustion and tedium and Lars exclaims that this is the shittiest job in existence. It is hot and wet even though they are down in a cool pit, and looking as if they are working with coal, or else it rains and they are wet and caked in mud down in the same hole doing battle with Hans's old cutting implements and throwing lumps of peat up onto the grass where there is no-one to stack them, every so often they have to climb up and do it themselves.

But then they hear the sound of Paulus's Bolinder motor and lay down their tools and climb up and make their way towards the quay at the same time as Ingrid and Barbro and Suzanne leave the house, they arrive together and discover that beside the empty milk churns on deck there are two ladies wearing capes and dresses. They recognise one of them, she is the priest's wife, Karen Louise Malmberget, as usual a delicate and radiant light in the Nordland day. But they don't recognise the other lady, she is Maria Helena Barrøy, who has returned from hospital with ashen hair and skin that looks as if it has never seen the sun as it belongs to a corpse in a grave.

But if they don't recognise her, she certainly recognises them, including Felix and Suzanne, who don't remember her. She walks slowly up onto the quay and lays a hand on their heads and smiles wearily, reacting with the same wan smile to the sobbing of Ingrid, who has buried her, together with her father, for good. Even Barbro has to turn away and see to the cart and churns.

Then Paulus steps onto the quay too, and asks if they have dried the fish and whether he can buy it at almost the same price as they pay at the Trading Post.

"Hvafor no' th' same?" Lars asks.

"Transportation," Paulus says.

"It's no' tha who pays f' th' oil," Lars says.

Paulus says he may well be right.

"Is it top quality, though?"

"Yes," Lars says.

Paulus says it is the graders who decide that.

Lars glances over at the unrecognisable Maria and sob-racked Ingrid, the homecomer has a nimbus around her no-one dares to encroach upon, then Ingrid takes her hand and leads her up to the house with the others in tow, Lars hears Karen Louise Malmberget tell Felix he – looks like th' Prince o' Darkness himself.

"Hvur did tha get s' black?"

Lars hears Felix laughing and turns to Paulus to say they will transport the stockfish themselves and sell it for what they pay at the Trading Post.

"Oh yes, has tha got money then?" Paulus asks, with a knowing look. Lars says they got a full catch share for the fishing gear they had in Lofoten in the winter. Paulus asks if they have already received the money. Lars says yes, Erling came over about a month ago and settled up, they have got the gear back and will repair it ready for next winter.

"Cash?" Paulus says in disbelief.

"Yes," Lars says, thinking the conversation is beginning to drag, he wants to follow the others and see whether he might be able to recognise Maria after all. But Paulus takes off his cloth cap and says he probably only has second-grade fish on his own drying rack.

"Bluebottles?" Lars asks.

"Yes."

"It's too hot o'er thar."

Paulus steps on board with a strange expression on his face.

241

Lars lifts off the hawsers and has something to ponder, he realises there is something he doesn't know, about the world and prices and not least the new owners of the Trading Post. So he doesn't go up to the house but to the boat shed where he launches the *færing* and sets off rowing in the direction of the main island and arrives at the Trading Post just as a coaster from Bergen docks, which creates a hustle and bustle on the wharf where people have actually left for the day.

He goes up the steps and loafs around like an inquisitive kid until he finds out that salted fish is to be loaded and that the new owner is a very young man, in his twenties. Lars has caught a glimpse of him once before and is surprised to see that he is dressed like one of the workers, whereas Tommesen always wore a tie and waistcoat, and that the only difference between the new owner and his workers is that he talks more loudly than them and has his hands in his pockets.

Lars seizes the opportunity as the grader walks between the stacked boxes of salted fish pointing out those the workers have to pull out and spread out across the floor of the salt house so that he can calculate what proportion of the fish is second-grade, a percentage which is applied to the whole consignment, a spot check. Lars has seen this before and knows it is a critical moment, for the finances of the Trading Post, the hazardous calculation at the end of a whole winter. Nevertheless he asks the owner of the Trading Post – Bang Johansen, he remembers he is called – whether he buys stockfish and, if so, at what price.

Bang Johansen peers down at Lars, but doesn't catch what

he says, his attention is focused on the grader who has pointed to a stack, and it seems to be a favourable selection, seen through Bang Johansen's eyes, a private smile flickers across his face, and he asks Lars to repeat the question, which he does, and Bang Johansen mumbles a sum and adds, as though reciting by rote, or reeling off some business patter, these are difficult times and transport is expensive, etc. But the price he gives is higher than Lars had dared to dream of, based on Paulus's information. He asks when he can deliver. Bang Johansen finally focuses on him and asks what he is talking about. Lars waits for him to ask the next question:

"Has tha fish?" Bang Johansen says.

"Yes."

"Tha from th' islands?"

"Yes."

"Well, tha'd bitter send tha father."

Lars is about to say "A *am* my father". But instead he waits until Bang Johansen once again realises he has said something stupid and says:

"Hvur much has tha got?"

"A don't know reit nu."

"O.K., just bring it."

"An' eider down? Does tha take down too?"

"Has tha down too?"

"Yes."

"Hvur much?"

"A don't know reit nu."

243

"O.K., just bring th' down an' we can have a look at it."

Lars is about to say that down from Barrøy is not something you look at, it is purer than gold, but he drops the idea too, he says:

"An' eggs?"

At this Bang Johansen laughs out loud and says he would be happy to take eggs as well.

"But hvur in hell did tha get s' black?"

On the way back home Lars is reminded of the question Hans once asked him while they were sitting in Scab Acre contemplating the new quay house and quay, one drowsy summer's evening when thoughts could span the whole firmament, had Lars thought about what was missing on Barrøy? Lars thought Barrøy was exactly as it should be. A boat, Hans said. With an engine. A smack. A cutter. A motorised boat at any rate. A quay made of rock, with a new quay house, looks stupid without a permanently moored vessel.

"It's a shi'e harbour," Lars had answered, it must have been last year some time, or the year before, he had just been told why the milk-run boat couldn't put in in stormy weather.

"But we've got rocks enough," Hans had continued, "t' make a mole five o' six yards out fro' the headland by th' Swedes' boathouse. That'd change th' current an' th' waves in th' sound."

Lars had thought a lot about this since his uncle died, and about the ruins in Karvika, with all its rocks, and sat visualising it as he rowed back home that evening, his meeting with Bang

Johansen also playing a part in his reasoning, the man with his hands in his pockets, who told him the price of stockfish. And even more ideas merged with the finely tuned rhythm of the oar strokes, the question of whether there might be other things that Barrøy needed, which it was now his job to discover, and do something about, if, for example, Barrøy was compared with other islands, or other places, the thought was mind-boggling, a whole winter's accumulated ideas, and nothing tangible to compare them with.

50

While Lars is at the Trading Post Ingrid is sitting in the kitchen looking at her mother, who has found her chair and in turn glances out of the window at her daughter and at the others, while smiling with thin, white lips and far too prominent cheekbones and says yes, please, to some coffee, as though she is visiting a foreign country, and to a *lefse*, which Barbro serves on Polish porcelain.

Maria picks up the cup and saucer, scrutinises them and nods as if she has become even more of a guest in her own house, otherwise she sits with her hands in her lap.

Ingrid walks in and out of the room, weeping when she is outside and smiling when she is back in.

Karen Louise follows her and says they have to talk, not about Maria's condition but about money. It appears that her father has a mortgage on the Barrøy property, farm registration number 55, title number 1, he has borrowed money before as well, on one occasion Pastor Malmberget has stood surety for a loan, he has always paid up, it isn't that, but now another instalment is due to Sparebanken, on July 1, a sum of three hundred kroner, they also have a considerable bill to pay at the

Store for items they received in the course of the winter, has Ingrid thought through what it would mean if the bank took over ownership of Barrøy, that may not be the worst option, they could buy a new plot on the main island, Karen Louise has already spoken to Paulus, he is no farmer and would be willing to sell, at a reasonable price, she says, blushing and breathless, and rounds off this grand plan by remarking what a terrible time they must have had this winter, she looks as if she is talking to a patient.

Ingrid cannot contradict this person, she is after all a sort of government in the parish, so Ingrid asks her to wait, goes up to the South Chamber and fetches three hundred of the kroner they were given by Uncle Erling, then goes back down, hands the money to Karen Louise Malmberget and asks if she would settle the instalment for her, with the bank, but as far as the bill at the Store is concerned it cannot be that much, they have paid cash all winter.

Karen Louise's cheeks go a deeper red.

Ingrid braces herself and says she would like Karen to sign a note that she has received this money and that it is to be paid to the bank and no-one else. Karen Louise asks where she got this large sum from and mumbles that a receipt is hardly necessary, is it?

Ingrid goes in and sits down beside her mother and asks what the two scars on her temples are. Maria smiles. Karen Louise follows her in, sits down, takes a sip of cold coffee, says no, thank you to Barbro, who offers her some more, and focuses

247

on Suzanne, who crawls up onto Ingrid's lap and steals a glance at Maria.

"Hvo's th' lady?" Suzanne asks.

"That's Mamma," Ingrid says, and moves Suzanne over to Maria's lap, goes to the chest of drawers in the sitting room, fetches paper and ink and sits down to write. Karen Louise reads the receipt disapprovingly and says she has forgotten the date, and what date it has to be paid. Ingrid writes the date. Karen Louise signs and says this really isn't necessary, and, oh, now she can hear the sound of Paulus's Bolinder.

But it isn't the milk run, it is the smooth oar strokes of Lars, who ties up the *færing*, comes up the slope, into the kitchen and looks around as though he has entered a tomb, and on the table he spots the receipt and the money.

"Hva's tha' thar?" he asks.

"Go an' have a wash," Ingrid says. "An' teik Felix with tha'."

"Hva's tha' thar?" Lars repeats.

Ingrid doesn't answer. Karen Louise thrusts the money into a brown leather bag decorated with green pearls. Ingrid folds the sheet of paper and sits waving it until Karen Louise gets up and tells Lars to come outside with her.

Ingrid watches them from the window, Lars walking beside the priest's wife towards the quay, stopping and opening his mouth and screaming something at her. Karen Louise covers her ears with her hands and leans forward. Lars continues to scream until she bends over further before straightening up and

248

hurrying towards the quay while Lars turns and races back to the house, into the kitchen, grabs the broomstick and smacks Ingrid across the head with it, causing her blood to spatter over the table and the receipt. She reels. She hears his voice. And sees Barbro wrapping her arms around him. He struggles and fights and yells. Ingrid staggers to her feet and feels the wound on her forehead, sees the blood, reaches for the broomstick and hits him twice on the forehead. Then Barbro screams too, pushes the boy aside and clasps her arms around Ingrid, who squirms and bites. Felix looks on, his eyes wide open. Suzanne smiles, a finger in her mouth. And Maria puts Suzanne down, stands up, walks towards the sink, grasps the pump handle and moves it back and forth, tastes the water and pumps faster and faster, Barbro lets go of Ingrid, throws her arms around Maria too and stops the water.

"Th' water, th' water . . ."

There is silence.

And Lars remembers he has to see to the fish, it is getting too warm outside. He heads for the drying-rack with Felix hard on his heels. Felix asks if the wound on his forehead hurts. Lars licks off the blood he can reach with his tongue and crawls under the rack, squints into the belly of fish after fish and sees neither fly eggs nor anything else untoward. Felix repeats the question. Lars doesn't answer, he makes a calculation, counts, and scans the island to make sure of something. He says:

"Let's go in t' Mamma an' get some hot water."

Over by the buildings he sees Ingrid and her mother coming

into the yard, Maria in a light-coloured dress, Ingrid in a dress too, she is holding her mother's hand as though she were a child – who is the child? – there comes Suzanne too, they walk towards the south of the island passing through the Acres causing a commotion amongst the birds, which soar up and swoop above them like fluttering white paper, Lars can hear their voices, but not what they are talking about, let's go in t' Barbro an' get some hot water, he says again to Felix.

51

They have two bits of business to attend to on the main island, the first is with the priest. Ingrid goes alone, against Lars's wishes, he and Felix watch over the *færing* with the stockfish and gulls' eggs while Ingrid sits in the rectory and receives a shock.

This is due to the priest's gentle yet merciless run-down of Hans's financial dealings over the years, not that her father had had a lot to juggle with on this earth, in Malmberget's view, Hans wanted not only to live on, but also to develop Barrøy, just as any heir wishes to leave more than he inherits, it is a cycle this is, a chain of life, a law. But this means that what Ingrid, throughout her life, has assumed to be an immovable rock in the sea has in truth been a rotting raft, which her father only just managed to keep afloat.

Ingrid sits transfixed in her chair wondering whether her mother has been informed of this, she also asks about this. The priest says he doesn't know, with a look that she interprets as indicating that she should ask others that question, whoever they may be.

To be on the safe side, Ingrid says no more.

Malmberget gets to his feet and walks around on noiseless carpets, serves her raspberry juice and himself coffee, sits down again, pulls out a drawer and gets to the point, namely that Ingrid is to receive a mortgage deed, some receipts and also her father's death certificate, together with the deeds of the property on Barrøy. Hereinafter it is she who is the rightful owner of Barrøy, the sole heir, since there are neither sons nor spouses of sound mind, this is a solemn procedure, a hint of something greater than themselves, which also makes its imprint on the silent room, where a nameless apostle looks down on them from his niche in the wall.

Ingrid is terrified.

But she also grows, inside, and reads everything that is written in the deeds, the listing of all the smaller and larger islands and skerries in her kingdom, as soon as she comes of age, uncultivated land, cultivated land, the rights to water and peat and berries and fishing and timber and flotsam . . . Gothic script, dotted lines, blue ink, black, elegant handwriting, red stamp . . .

The priest asks how her mother is doing.

Ingrid looks up and thinks.

She says she doesn't know, she doesn't sleep in the same room anymore, but with Suzanne and the cat in the South Chamber, Maria is alone in Ingrid's old room. In the daytime she sits in the kitchen or on a chair in the sunshine, the way Barbro used to do, and only occasionally goes to the cowshed, and very seldom cooks, slowly, they have to get her started an hour earlier . . .

The priest nods.

We have too many cows, Ingrid says, and too little land. And we need a horse. She has done her calculations, based on the fact that her father was a human machine, who was able to mow five acres with the scythe, last year Lars couldn't even manage one, Barbro was hard put to do half an acre and Maria a quarter. They could harness one of the cows to the old mower, but it was a lot of work and they would lose the milk, they could also use a cow to pull the plough in the potato field if they only used the coulter and mouldboard, and then there was the relative proportion of pasture and cultivated land, it wasn't as it should be . . .

Pastor Malmberget feels he can discern a calculation here, whereby the pluses and minuses of different strategies have been carefully weighed up, Ingrid has been seeking the golden formula for running Barrøy, the optimal ratio between animals and land and people and sea, a delicate balance which has to be tended with care so that a certain number of people are able to live there, no fewer and no more, exactly the number of people who live there now in fact, and he smiles.

They arrive at a kind of summing-up. He praises her maturity and opens the drawer once again – by way of a concluding exhortation – and slides some more documents across the table – duplicates of two birth certificates, Felix's and Suzanne's – and adds that she will have to make sure that Felix starts school in the autumn, on Havstein, he, Johannes Malmberget, has already taken the liberty of enrolling him.

Ingrid gets up and agrees, even though she knows it is going to be difficult, if she has become a mother in the course of the year, Lars has become a father, and how! And he himself has no plans to go back to the classroom.

But her stature has not diminished as a result of this meeting.

She curtsies, reflecting that even though she hasn't dared to bring up the most difficult issue, and the priest didn't either, a resolution of the children's future, it hasn't come any closer as a result of these two duplicate birth certificates, which she puts into the envelope together with the title deeds and the proof that her father is dead.

Lars and Felix have walked up from the Trading Post and are sitting on the coke bin outside the Store, and Lars thinks he can see a spring in Ingrid's step as she comes down from the rectory, the envelope squeezed under her arm, she looks like a school-mistress. He jumps down and asks whether they'll be getting the boat then, with the engine, whether they can they afford it now, will the priest be a guarantor . . .?

Ingrid says they aren't getting a boat, they're getting a horse.

"A horse?!"

Lars has never heard anything so stupid, they have had a horse before, it worked for one month, then stopped and stuffed its face for eleven.

"Is tha goen' t' mow all Barrøy?" she says. "Wi' a scythe?"

Lars has no answer to that. Ingrid says they are going to borrow a horse.

"One o' Adolf's in Malvika. He's got three."

"Hvur's it goen' t' get hier, swim?"

Ingrid explains that Paulus will ship over the horse the same way he transports cows and breeding bulls.

"An' tha' won' cost much, will it," Lars says.

"But we're only haven' two cows."

"Hvafor?"

She explains that two cows produce just enough milk for the milk run to keep coming to their island, they are dependent on this now. But she fails to mention that the boat can also be used for school transport, and also omits to inform him about another part of the calculation, with only two cows there will be less to do in the cow barn, Barbro can make nets and Ingrid can prepare them and pick berries and . . . all the rest, while Maria . . . she doesn't mention her mother either.

"An' we're goen' t' have meir sheep."

From now on the sheep will be grazing for a shorter time on Barrøy, and longer on Skogsholmen, Knuten and Gjesøya, from when the snow melts until as long as possible after the snow returns.

Lars hasn't much to say about this either, they have arrived at the Trading Post and are about to attend to their second business matter.

Lars manoeuvres the *færing* under the crane. The barrel of

eggs, which is a ton weight, is hoisted ashore, and then the dried fish. Bang Johansen hears the clatter on the wharf and comes out to see what is going on.

He also wants to test the eggs in water, so he removes the barrel lid, scrapes a little sand aside and picks out four black-backed gulls' eggs and two eider-duck eggs, and all of them sink as they should, but he has put them in a rinsing tank, not a bucket, it is almost a metre deep, he has to lean over the edge and plunge halfway down to get them out again, so the top part of his body gets soaked. They laugh at him, he smiles and asks:

"Hvur many eggs has tha in th' barrel?"

"Eighty," Lars says.

"Has tha meir?"

"One meir barrel. Comen' tomorrow."

Bang Johansen nods and sets about inspecting the dried fish, which they have stacked on a pallet, and finds no fault with them either. But the price has gone down since last time, due to the market . . .

"Bastard," Felix says.

"Hva war that?"

Felix is about to repeat it. Ingrid cuffs him round the ear.

"He doesn't e'en know hva it means."

"A do too," Felix says, and gets another cuff. Lars smiles down at the planks on the wharf and Bang Johansen shakes his head and says little brat and casts his eye over the fish again and asks what it is going to be. Ingrid asks him to weigh the fish and make them out a chit, and also a ticket for the eggs. He weighs them with all eyes on him and arrives at the same number of kilos as they had, with their steelyard. And he gives them the two receipts.

"But hva about th' down?"

Ingrid keeps her composure and tells Bang Johansen they can talk about the down later.

"Hvafor?"

The manner in which he asks, his eyes and face. Does he really want the down, she asks. He says of course. She has seen this before, with her father, then the merchant would just give a fixed price, which her father said yes or no to, then left, empty-handed if necessary. She asks what the price of down is this year. Bang Johansen tells her. She repeats that she will think about it, first they will have to bring in the rest of the fish, which will take three or four days, and the eggs. Bang Johansen nods.

"Yes, reit, th' eggs."

On the way back to the island Felix and Lars take the oars, Ingrid sits on the aft thwart with a brown envelope on her lap, feeling the balmy summer breeze in her hair.

"Hva ar' tha grinnen' a'?" Lars says.

"Nothin'," says the queen of Barrøy, who is being rowed out to her kingdom by two subjects who have no idea what plans she has, nor will they get to hear of them before they are implemented. She has learned this from her father. Silence. The element of surprise. The deeds and the duplicates in the envelope. No, she has learned this from her mother. Or has she? She can't remember. She is no longer smiling. She misses them both more now than she has ever done since they died. And Lars looks away.

52

Hans Barrøy had three dreams: he dreamed about a boat with a motor, about a bigger island and a different life. He mentioned the first two dreams readily and often, to all and sundry, the last he never talked about, not even to himself.

Maria had three dreams too: more children, a smaller island and – a different life. Unlike her husband she often thought about the last of these, and this yearning grew and grew as the first two paled and withered.

When her husband died she began to have regrets.

To regret having a dream is the most debilitating experience there is. She regretted thinking the island was too big, with all the endless work it entailed, and wishing for more children, because she had Ingrid.

Thereafter a threat slowly unfurled inside her, the feeling from the time when the convict had been there and stolen something they didn't know they had, and left a stain on their lives, something came with the wind, the birds and the sea, the snow, the water in the kitchen and the eagles that had begun to sit on the roof of the quay house. She could hear the thudding of the cat's paws across the floor, which compounded into a solid drop that swelled and contracted like an animal's heart.

I'll take you by the hand, Mamma, Ingrid says, standing in the doorway of her childhood room, waiting for Maria to get up and dress.

They go down to the kitchen and drink coffee and have breakfast, which Barbro has put on the table. Barbro has already attended to the animals, they are in the fields round the clock now, and come bellowing to the buildings when their udders are bursting and wake anyone who is listening, and this summer it is Barbro, Barbro who curses and gets up and milks them, Ingrid is busy with other things.

Ingrid goes back upstairs and wakes Suzanne, watches as she gets dressed as well, in the clothes she herself once wore, goes down and finishes eating and then into the fields, whatever the weather.

They walk around the island and see that the grass has grown and know that it will get taller yet. They row over to the islets and count the lambs. Maria recognises some things, but not all, she says, ah, yes, and sees something even Ingrid can't remember. She asks how many children she has. Ingrid says three. No, Maria says. She articulates single words, as if to practise saying them, boat, lighthouse, horse ... Here come the children, she says as the *færing* returns after the day's trip to the Trading Post with stockfish. Ingrid shouts, you remembered the receipt, didn't you? Lars doesn't answer, climbs up the ladder and heads home to get something to eat, with Felix close on his heels.

Maria's smile.

It doesn't belong here.

They sit down on the quay and she recalls how her husband was dressed when they met, what he said, his ideas, and Ingrid's eyelids droop, but she lets her continue, the horse, the sand, the fireplace . . . Suzanne throws stones into the sea and balances on the edge of the quay. Ingrid tells her to stop. Maria comments on how lovely the young girl looks, with her hair combed and groomed like a doll, and Ingrid realises that the littl'un would probably make herself dirty if she got Maria's attention, that Suzanne is beginning to know how to exploit her charms. This evening she will be going with them to do the milking, the cows are in Bosom Acre now, where the mower can't be used anyway, the grass is getting even higher, the most peaceful days of the year merge into one another, without nights, while the grass grows and the rain falls and the sun shines and the gulls scream, until Paulus comes with the horse.

It is spring high tide and midnight, all the sounds inside a glass flask, the voice of the light nights. Ingrid can see Maria's eyes change at the sight of the horse, which Paulus has tied by its legs and upper body and head to the railing, the wheelhouse and the mast, it stands locked into position like a wooden toy and has deposited a huge pile of shit on the deck.

They push out the gangway that Felix and Lars have made,

the animal is led ashore and will stay on Barrøy until the next spring tide, some time in the dog days, Ingrid has calculated, so it will have time to plough up new ground for potatoes next summer.

Paulus also delivers a consignment of goods from the Store. Ingrid wants to make sure that everything is as it should be, but again she notices Maria's eyes, sees she has placed a hand on the horse's mane as if to welcome the animal, and her eyes roll, she bends her neck and sways, her hand grabbing the mane, it keeps her upright, she lifts her head and gazes at Ingrid with eyes that have stopped rolling. And Ingrid wants to loosen her grip and take her home, but Maria lets go herself, pats the horse's neck and says:

"They shot th' horse."

"Hva?"

"They shot th' horse an' thought we didn't see."

The others lead the horse away. Maria and Ingrid walk home and sit on the rainwater-tank lid. Maria with the midnight sun shining through her hair, turning it completely white, it can't even be plaited. She says she has spoken to Zezenie at the hospital, several times, or tried, she won't be back.

Ingrid nods.

"Does tha get hva A'm sayen'?"

"Yes," Ingrid says.

Maria asks if she has settled everything with the priest, the papers?

Ingrid nods.

"Good."

Ingrid asks if she wants to move back to the South Chamber. Maria answers no, there is no need. She says she wanted to talk to the doctors about the thudding cat's paws, but they only wanted to hear about her husband, and she remembered just one episode, he wanted to sit directly opposite her at the kitchen table so as not to lose her for a single second, it was only a year ago he said that, or two. Then she fell asleep and didn't wake up again until she placed her hand on a horse and felt its muscles breathing under its hot skin. Ingrid says she understands, but she is worried and asks her mother if she believes her father knew he was going to die. Maria deliberates, and says no, it was a good death, he died when he had to die, it is like so much else that is good, it is impossible to know.

53

The horse was called Wilhelm after a Kaiser and wasn't like the one they had before, in the first place it didn't mind being on an island, and it didn't kick, but it was lazy and good-natured, and lay down to sleep when they unharnessed it from whatever it had been pulling. Felix and Suzanne could ride it.

With it came two buckets of linseed oil, one small and one large sack of powder, and some brushes, Ingrid wanted to paint the house.

'Th' hus is goen' t' bi white."

With green windows and barge boards.

When they weren't mowing and drying the hay, they were painting. Maria too. She painted the windows, slowly and painstakingly. This was the first house on Barrøy to see any paint. And it changed not only the house but also the whole island, it transformed the rocks and sand and grass and animals and trees. When they had finished they couldn't look at it, at any rate they couldn't believe what they saw, the old grey house looked as if it had been cast out of freshly fallen snow, it seemed to be located somewhere else, on the mainland, in a town, it smacked of immense wealth, resplendent here in all its glory, without rivals, it was a shock, a foreign body, it was enough to make you split your sides with laughter.

They went into the fields in the evening and turned around and looked homeward and thought that is where we live. This was also the first thing they did in the morning: go out and look at the house, it gave them energy, hope, and put them in a good mood. It was nicer to be outside than in, and it hadn't been like that before. The house looked different when viewed from Love Spinney from how it did from Frosteye or Karvika, it was changeable and volatile and visible from the other islands, a tower, a landmark in the sea, an icon. People came by in their rowing boats and wondered what the Barrøy islanders had been getting up to now, asked whether the paint was expensive and durable and difficult to apply, before rowing home again, their heads full of ideas.

The house was visible all the way from the Trading Post. It was visible from the sky, from the sea, from the mountains on the mainland, from the government offices in Oslo, and Borneo, there wasn't an eye that couldn't see it.

They hitched up the lazy horse to the mower and cut the grass in Rose Acre and Scab Acre and the Garden of Eden. They found all the old holes for the drying-rack posts and erected the racks the way they had always been, north to south, so they wouldn't be blown down, undulating grey-green lines criss-crossing the stone walls.

In the course of the summer there were many developments they hadn't dared hope for. Uncle Erling paid a visit with his family and allied himself with Ingrid with regard to schooling; Lars would have to arm himself with patience for another year before they would take him with them to Lofoten. Aunt Helga couldn't recognise Maria, and couldn't hide her disappointment, her all too obvious disappointment. She didn't recognise Suzanne or Felix either, the little girl was in nappies the last time she had seen her, and chubby Felix had become as thin as a rake and looked older than the eight years he would soon be, according to the duplicate birth certificate which bore his name, a name which was to be changed as soon as Ingrid found the time, from Tommesen to Barrøy.

When Paulus comes to collect the horse they have finally realised what their forefathers had always known, a horse can only be a temporary guest on an island, it has something to do with the size of the place, which can be difficult to come to terms with, it is all bound up with grass and money and ambitions and work and divine calculations.

Eventually they decide to mow the reclaimed land on Gjesøya too.

It has to be done with scythes.

The whole family joins in. They discuss whether to have drying racks here too. Ingrid says they should. Lars disagrees. Ingrid says it is easier to transport dry hay than wet. Lars says that in that case they would have to row poles and cords both ways, and sledgehammers and crowbars. Maria agrees with

Ingrid. Suzanne does too. Barbro sides with Lars. So does Felix. Ingrid says that school will be starting soon. Felix says he is looking forward to it. Lars says nothing. There are two camps. One of them usually gets its way. And on a hot, late summer day a grey *haar* suddenly forms like a wall on the horizon and slowly creeps towards them, leaving one island after the other in blue-grey darkness, swallowing up and enveloping everything and everyone in a cold, raw blanket. Where previously they had an unimpeded view in all directions, now they cannot even see their own sheep, neither can they see the hay-drying racks or the bushes or the lighthouse or the gleaming house on Barrøy, only a few blades of grass right in front of their feet and the tears rolling down them, even though it isn't raining.

The *haar* brings its gloom in the middle of the day, a solar eclipse and a loss of vision. They put down their tools in silence and wrap themselves up in warmer clothes, sit on a rock and let their thoughts roam free, illuminated by an inner light – just as the blind look inwards because they have no alternative – and come upon a memory or a wisp of something no-one understands and which they cannot share or put to any use.

When vision is lost the other senses become keener, the intense smell of nettles and marshland and seaweed and wet wool, the *haar* as salty as the sea that engendered it, a stranger's cold embrace on the skin, and even though the eider duck rises and spreads its wings above the ground, and insects and animals are as silent as the people here, a strange sound emanates from inside the *haar*, a rushing sound, like the ocean in a conch shell or a dead rat being dragged through powdery snow.

But no more than an hour or two passes before the sun burns it all away, at first a boiled cod eye in the haze a few degrees further north, then yellower and more golden until it dispels and destroys the last remaining shroud, thereby unleashing their vision in all directions, like wild horses. Then it is as though they have had their working day halved, or been given a whole new day within the old one, and can set to work with the scythe again.

ROY JACOBSEN has twice been nominated for the Nordic Council's Literary Award: for *Seierherrene* in 1991 and *Frost* in 2003. In 2009 he was shortlisted for the Dublin Impac Award for his novel *The Burnt-Out Town of Miracles*. *The Unseen* was a phenomenal bestseller in Norway.

DON BARTLETT is the acclaimed translator of books by Karl Ove Knausgård, Jo Nesbø and Per Petterson.

DON SHAW, co-translator, is a teacher of Danish and author of the standard Danish–Thai/Thai–Danish dictionaries.